Lexi Lets Go

Mystic Falls

Mary Warren

To my exhausted readers, you deserve rest. You're allowed to rest before everything is done. You're allowed to rest before everything is perfect. Go take a nap.

Foreword

Hello,

Thank you so much for giving Lexi and Liam a try, before you read I wanted to share a content warning

Content Warnings

- Explicit Sexual Content
- Childhood Neglect
- Childhood Death of a Parent
- Parental Alcoholism
- Media Scandal involving Fatphobia and LGBTQ issues

If you are good to go I hope you enjoy this love story about learning to let go and accept the love you deserve.

Prologue

Sweat dripped off Liam's body as he left the stage. He had played his set and the last encore in the scorching heat. The energy of the audience had kept him going, but now he was about to collapse. He grabbed a water bottle someone put in his hand and drained it. Some of the water spilled out of his mouth intermingling with the sweat that already soaked through his shirt.

"You have someone in your trailer, Mr. James," said a stagehand as they handed him another bottle of water.

"Thanks," he said as he walked toward his trailer. "Make sure you're staying hydrated too, it's a scorcher," he called back to the stagehand.

"Thank you, Mr. James."

Liam made his way through the dust-covered rows of trailers until he came to his.

"Liam," his manager called, "You have time for a quick shower and maybe a short nap. Once the buses are loaded up we are hitting the road. I left some food in your refrigerator when you want it. I'll be by to get you when we are ready. Probably ninety minutes or so."

"Thanks, Jacinda. I'll be ready," he said as he climbed the steps to his trailer. He opened the door and there sitting at the table was a short round woman with wild red hair.

"Hello Mr. James, I was told ye wanted to see me," she said in a thick Scottish brogue. Her eyes twinkled with a knowing look as she shuffled the cards in her hand.

"Yeah, thanks for coming over. I heard you tell a good fortune," he said with his million-dollar smile.

"I've been known to tell a fortune or two in my day," she quipped.

She gestured to the empty chair and Liam sat. "Now, what is it yer wanting the cards to tell ye?"

His mind raced. What didn't he want the cards to tell him? Even though he was only twenty-six, he was one of the most successful performers on the planet. He loved his job, he loved his music, and above all else he loved his fans, but something was still missing. It felt like he had just been going through the motions. He still loved performing, but he hadn't written anything in over a year. He had lost his inspiration. He was willing to try anything at this point, and this delightful woman across from him might be able to guide him back to his muses.

"I'm just trying to find my muse again. My creativity is blocked," he said as he ran his hand through his sweat-dampened hair.

"I see, well let's see what the cards have to say about that." The woman started shuffling a well-loved tarot deck. "Cut the cards, lad," she said, setting the cards on the table before. After he did, she picked the cards up and started flipping.

"The first card will represent your past." The card had a large heart with three large swords all stabbed into it. "Oh my," she said, giving him a sympathetic look, "The Three of

Swords is a card of heartbreak and loneliness, but also one of betrayal. Someone has not had your best interest at heart, and it appears to have caused you some heartbreak."

Liam just nodded. He'd had his fair share of heartbreak, but that was public knowledge. That is what his whole album was about. The heartbreak that had all been caused because of a very public scandal.

"This next card will represent your present," she said as she turned over the next card. There on the card before him sat a skeleton riding a horse and holding a giant sickle. The death card.

"Never fear, dear. This card may look big and scary, but this is quite possibly my favorite card in the deck. This is a card of transformation. A card of leaving behind things that no longer serve you and getting a new beginning. A fresh start to maybe recovering from the heartache and loneliness of this card," she said pointing to the card next to it.

"Now let's see what the future holds," she said as she held up a third card. She looked at it and hummed with a content smile. Before her lay a hand stretching out from the clouds holding a single stave. "Never fear lad, your muse will be returning to you shortly."

"Really?" he asked, maybe there was some hope after all.

"That's what the cards say, this card is a renewed sense of energy. You will find your north star, and you will steer your own ship with renewed energy," she said with such certainty, Liam found himself hoping it was true.

"So, I know things have been broken down, life is full of heartaches, but I think you will find the perfect spot for renewal, wash it all away in the rain and the waterfall, and then you will find what you need for your next phase. I think you will find a new love to be your inspiration. Then

I think the creativity will flow but will be different this time."

That may not have made sense to him, but for the first time in a long time, he was hopeful. He had a few more shows, then he would spend a month at home with his family in Ohio before getting ready for the last leg of his tour which would end in NYC in the summer. After that, he didn't know what was next, but if this lovely woman in front of him was correct, his muse would return, and he would know the direction to take things.

After his reading and his shower, Liam got on his tour bus heading to the next city. He had been told to watch who he trusted and be on the lookout for love. It seemed like pretty stereotypical advice to tell a person in his situation. And as much as he loved being in love, his life right now just didn't allow for it. Still, he did find himself pondering her words late into the night as he lay in his bed strumming his guitar as they barreled down the highway.

Chapter 1

Lexi

The inn door shut behind Lexi as she made her way to her car. She looked at her watch. Six o'clock. Not bad. She had been staying late at work the past couple of weeks. Okay, that was a lie, she had been staying late at work since her promotion a couple of years ago. She knew this inn backwards and forwards, and she found some sense of fulfillment here. If she was being honest, it was a good thing because that fulfillment was missing from every other part of her life.

She made her way to her car and flung her lunch bag and purse onto the passenger seat. Putting the keys in the ignition she heard her phone beep in her purse. She wasn't even out of the parking lot, surely it wasn't work yet, and if it wasn't work there was only one other person it could be... well, two people.

Josh- Hey Lex, I know it's short notice, but I'm tossing some pork chops on the grill. I have one here with your name on it.

> Lexi- Thanks, but I'm just gonna cozy up at home tonight.

> Josh- You sure? We would love to have you.

> Lexi- I appreciate it, but I'm sure. Next time.

> Josh- Next Time! For real Lexi, I haven't seen you in weeks.

> Lexi- You just got married three months ago. Aren't you guys still in your honeymoon phase? You don't need me hanging around.

> Josh- Yes, but I still miss my sister. You are coming over this weekend or I am coming over there. End of story.

> Lexi- deal.

Slipping her phone back into her purse, she started on her way home. Life had changed for her in the past six months. Her whole life, it had always been her and her brother against the world. The two of them were all the family they had left and had always leaned on each other heavily. But three months ago, her baby brother had gotten married, and while she was nothing but thrilled for him, it had changed things.

She loved Poppy, and she loved seeing Josh happy, but things were just different. Her life used to be: work as hard as she could, take care of her baby brother and figure the rest out. Now she was still working as hard as she could, but she didn't need to take care of her brother. She hadn't really had to take care of him in years. He was just as hardworking and independent as she was. And in the past couple years she had grown to lean on him just as much as he had leaned on her. He was someone to call when her car wouldn't start, a warm meal on the table after working back-to-back shifts. But now it was just her.

She missed feeling like she was in this with someone else. When he was younger, she had taken care of him because someone needed to. So, she just did it. She had been in survival mode since she was young, and that kind of thinking was hard to shake.

Once she was home and showered, she put some comfy pajamas on. She then went to the freezer to figure out what was for dinner that night. She picked the least objectionable microwave dinner, she got it out, poked the plastic film, and put it in the microwave. The stack of mail on the kitchen table was growing into a mound. Pulling out the bills and the important looking mail she swept the rest into the recycle bin and poured herself a glass of wine. After the microwave dinged, she got her frozen dinner and her glass of wine and went to watch TV.

As she looked down at what the box had called chicken and broccoli, she was kicking herself for turning down Josh's invitation for dinner. He was a fantastic cook, sure she missed him, but she might have missed his food even more. She somehow managed to eat her dinner, if she was even going to call it that, drank another glass of wine and watched a couple reruns before turning into bed.

In her bedroom, she plugged her phone in and made sure the alarm was set. She pulled up the romance novel she was currently reading and settled into bed. She wasn't sure why she read these books. She had never been in what most people would consider a real relationship. There had been some purely physical encounters over the years, but she had just never taken the time to get to know anyone new. It might be time to start, but after a lifetime of keeping everyone at arm's length, she wasn't really sure how to go about letting people in.

Next time Josh invited her over, she would go. She told herself that every time, but then he would message her, and she would say no and go home to her sad Lean Cuisine. She wasn't even sure why she was pushing him away. It was time to make a change. Maybe make a friend that wasn't her brother. Making life changes in your thirties however, is much easier said than done, but that was a problem for another day.

The next morning Lexi swatted her nightstand trying to turn off her phone's alarm. It was time for another day in Mystic Falls. Which would be just like yesterday in Mystic Falls, which would be just like tomorrow in Mystic Falls. She got ready for work and decided to stop at the diner for breakfast on her way to the inn, at least that would be a little bit of novelty for the day.

As she walked in, she could tell people were all a twitter about something, she chuckled thinking what it might be. Last month a raccoon had gotten into Fipp's Market over the night and had made a mess of things and just walked right out when Mr. Fipp came to open the store, like the fat and sassy raccoon he was. That caused quite the hubbub for a week. Lexi wondered what it might be now. A cow in the town square? High school students making out behind the theater?

Sitting in her usual booth, she decided she might stay for an actual breakfast today instead of her usual coffee and muffin to go. Mae made her way over to the table and brought her a menu.

"Good morning, Lexi. I haven't seen you in a while. Are you eating here this morning?"

"Yeah, I have a little time. What's going on? Everyone seems a bit more excitable than usual."

"Well, ya know, it's kind of interesting," Mae said, giving her a conspiratorial look. "Sometime last night this large tour bus broke down. No one is really sure why it's here or what's going on with it."

"Tour bus?" Lexi asked, "What do you mean?"

"One of those big buses just pulled over on the side of the road over on the south end of town."

"Hmmm... Interesting. Can I have a ham and cheese omelet?" Lexi asked.

"Coming right up." Mae left the table and Lexi watched with an amused smile as Vivian Williams and Ms. Maple sat in the booth by the door sharing whispers and keeping the cogs of this town's gossip machine well oiled. Looking out the window she spotted one of Mystic Falls newest faces, Bridget from the magic shop in town. She smiled at Lexi as she walked past the diner. Lexi waved back and she nodded her head as she passed by. She had done a card reading for Lexi a few months ago and Lexi had been thinking about it for a long time. She didn't hold much stock in magic, but there was something about that woman made her question it.

Ms. Maple gasped and pointed out the window. Vivian turned almost all the way around in her seat to look. But then Lexi saw what they saw. It was a large group of people walking towards the diner. There were probably ten people all coming their way. Half of them were staring down and furiously texting on their phones, but in the middle of all of it was a man she recognized, but she couldn't figure out where from. Definitely not from Mystic Falls.

They all came bustling into the diner as Mae brought Lexi her breakfast. Mae's eyes were huge, and Lexi could see the panic setting in.

"Find a seat where you can, I will be right with you all," Mae said.

"Do you have a meeting room here?" asked one of the women who barely glanced up from her phone.

"Ummm... No, I'm sorry ma'am. We can move some tables together if you'd like."

The woman looked up at her with utter irritation.

"I'm sorry," Mae said at a loss.

"That's alright ma'am," said the captivating man who was right in the center of the chaos. "We'll just get some breakfast and then find a place to work. Our bus broke down and needs to be worked on."

Who was this guy? He looked so familiar to her. He stood there calm in the middle of the storm all around him. He had on some ripped baggy jeans, chucks, a tight plain white t-shirt, and oversized sunglasses. A mess of brown perfectly tousled locks rested on top of his head.

"If you guys are looking for a workspace while your bus gets fixed, we have a meeting room at the inn. I think it is open today. Let me double check," said Lexi.

The crowd of people turned toward her. "That would be good. Do you have wifi?" asked the woman in front with her hair pulled tightly back into a long perfect ponytail.

Lexi stopped digging through her purse and looked up at the woman. Was she serious? This may be a small town, but it wasn't stuck in time, but by judging the serious and annoyed look on her face, she meant it.

"Yes, we have wifi." Lexi shook her head as she texted

her front desk to see if there was availability. "And our meeting room is open today. Just head over after breakfast and we'll get you guys set up."

The woman just nodded. How rude.

"Hey, thanks a lot," a velvety smooth voice said. "When it comes time to charge us, go ahead and double it. We will be out of your hair as soon as we can get back on the road."

When she looked up, she realized it was coming from the guy who had been surrounded by the flock of busy people. As she looked at him her mouth fell slack. He pushed his sunglasses up onto his head and smiled at her. Lexi's heart stopped beating for a moment, and she felt blood rushing to her head, and other places blood had no right to rush at eight AM on a Wednesday morning.

He walked over to her and put his hand out. Lexi just stared at him blankly. Vivian Williams cleared her throat loudly, snapping her out of her trance. She put her hand out to shake his.

"I'm Liam, nice to meet you -" he paused waiting for her name.

Lexi just looked at him as he inclined his head like he was waiting for a response, all while his devastatingly charming smile never left his face. She needed to respond, but to what? She couldn't think of what to say. As her brain caught up, she closed her eyes and shook her head.

"I'm Lexi," she said.

"Well, Lexi, nice to meet you."

"Nice to meet you too...." she trailed off, eyes locked on his.

"Liam," he said, clearly amused by their exchange.

"Yes, Liam. It is nice to meet you. Well, I better head over to the inn and make sure everything is set up for you all."

Lexi stood up and grabbed her purse. Turning, she walked right out of the diner. It wasn't until she was halfway to the inn when she realized her car was still back at the diner, along with her breakfast, which she did not pay for. What the hell just happened? And who was that guy?

Chapter 2

Liam

This morning Liam had awoken to a loud bang and a jolt on his tour bus, only to find out the bus carrying him and his staff had been separated from the bus with his equipment and roadies by over a hundred miles. They were stuck in this town that seemingly popped up out of nowhere.

After they had gotten the bus to the garage to fix, he noticed a shop that was about a block down. While his manager was dealing with the bus, he walked down to check it out.

It was a small magic shop. Peering in the window he looked in and saw one wall with baskets filled with little crystals and jars upon jars of dried herbs. On the other side of the wall were bookshelves filled with books on witchcraft and tarot cards and many other goodies. In the middle of the space was a small table with chairs. Something about this space called to him, and he wasn't sure why.

"Can I help ye, Lad?" asked a kind Scottish voice from behind him.

He turned to see an older woman with curly red hair. "No, I'm just taking a little walk while my bus gets fixed."

"Oh no, your bus broke down, did it? That's too bad. Will it be long?" she asked with a grin like the Cheshire Cat.

"I'm not actually sure yet."

"Well, if you are looking for breakfast Mae's diner a few blocks in town makes a great omelet."

"Thanks, I just might check that out. Is this your shop?" he asked as he watched her turn the key and enter carrying a cup of tea and bag, probably from the said diner. The more he looked at her, the more familiar she seemed. "I'm sorry, have we met?"

"Aye, I believe I read your cards a few months back at that music festival in New Mexico."

"Yes! I remember you. I'm still looking for my muse," he said to her with a joking smile and a raised eyebrow.

"Well, why don't you go get breakfast, maybe you'll find her there. Have a nice day!"

And just like that she disappeared behind the door. There was something about this woman he couldn't quite put his finger on. She seemed to know things, and it was a bit unsettling.

He continued down the picturesque main street lined with charming stores. A few blocks down he could see a town square. He had been hoping to find a small town with the right vibe for a video for his single Home, and this place might be just what he's been looking for.

His assistant came walking towards him looking angry. "Well, it looks like it is going to take a little while to get the bus running again. I am going to fire that driver. I have no clue how we ended up here away from everyone else."

"No need to fire him, let's just find out what happened. Should we go get some breakfast?"

"Where? We are in the middle of nowhere."

"Well, it looks like we are in the middle of a charming little town. I'm told there is a diner down a couple blocks. Let's go give it a shot," he said warmly.

"Fine, maybe they will have a meeting room so I can start trying to get this all sorted."

"How many small town diners have you been to, Jacinda?"

"Ummm... none."

"Let's go," he said as he pulled her and the rest of his team along. Sometimes he wished he didn't have to be such a spectacle, but that was just the way of things when you were as famous as he was. Being famous had its advantages, but it also meant having to travel with a crew when you're on the road.

The crew for his first album had been smaller; it was just his old manager, a few roadies and the band. He kind of missed the good old days. He missed his old manager, and the ease of life back then. But then he would think of his fans. The Liam James culture was one of joy and acceptance. He worked to create community in all of his shows that celebrated living one's own truth out loud with joy. That is how he used to live his life, but lately things had changed for him. He hadn't written anything in well over a year, ever since everything went terribly wrong right after his first tour ended. The label had killed the scandal, but there had been a cost. The more control they took over his image, the more he felt lost in it.

As they came into the diner, Liam could already feel all eyes on him. He was familiar with small towns and how fast word got around. Not that he really minded.

He heard Jacinda ask for a meeting room and he couldn't help but chuckle to himself. She really was clueless about the way these places worked. She was a great manager but was born and raised in LA, so this was probably pretty foreign to her. Her father was a lawyer for Liam's label and that is how he ended up hiring her. She did a good job, and she was no nonsense, which Liam appreciated.

When they entered the diner, his eyes had immediately been pulled to this woman. She was sitting at a table by herself. She had shoulder-length blonde hair cut in a sensible bob. Her outfit was business casual, but he did take note of the cleavage peeking out due to her ample chest. Her most striking feature was her deep blue eyes. They looked like the kind of eyes that could cut through all the bullshit and see right down to a person's core.

Then this woman spoke and offered them a meeting room at her inn. His intrigue for this woman was growing by the minute. He introduced himself to her and she seemed flustered. He was used to that. Most people he met were flustered by him, it came with the territory. But he wasn't used to feeling flustered as well. This woman with the most beautiful eyes had been drawing him in, it was like he felt a magnetic pull towards her.

After their brief exchange of pleasantries, she just stood up and left. She didn't pay or even take a bite of the tasty looking omelet she had ordered. While odd, he was used to people doing things like that around him. She must be a fan. That thought made him smile.

Beside the pull he felt to her and her striking eyes, there was something about her body that he just wanted to look at. She was short and round and looked so soft. He bet she would feel as good as the squishmallows he got from his younger fans. The way her very generous ass swayed as she dashed out of the diner pulled him up short.

He hadn't felt this kind of instant attraction in a long time. Being an artist, getting swept away in emotions was just a part of it. But this was not an emotion that had stirred in him for a very long time. He was going to find some time before he slipped away to talk to her. Just talk to her. But his mind was definitely doing more than talking to her.

Chapter 3

Lexi

The walk to the inn wasn't long, but it was long enough to break the spell that guy she had been put under. She also made a mental note to call Mae later and apologize for leaving without paying. That had to be one of the weirdest reactions she had ever had to someone, and she didn't even know who he was. I mean she knew he was somebody, you kind of have to be to have an entourage like that, but she couldn't place him. She should text Poppy. This was information her sister-in-law would definitely either have or be dying to have.

When she pulled the door of the inn open, Nancy came barreling towards her. There was something comical about this woman in her late fifties with curly red hair piled on top of her head running to the door.

"Is it true?" she asked.

"Is what true?"

"Liam James! Is it true he's in Mystic Falls?" asked Nancy with barely contained glee.

Lexi blinked for a moment before all the pieces clicked

in her mind. "Yes! Liam James, he's a singer, right? I thought that he looked familiar."

"Wait. You met him?" she asked with her jaw on the floor.

"Yes, and you probably will too. He and his team of people will be using the meeting room today until their bus is fixed."

"He's coming here?" Nancy asked as she instantly started smoothing her shirt and pants and checking her hair in the window reflection.

"Yes, he is. Maybe you should call your husband and four children and tell them," Lexi said with a joking smile.

"I've just never met anyone famous before, and to believe he is right here in Mystic Falls. Who would have thought?"

"Nancy, correct me if I'm wrong, but isn't your son a pretty famous NHL player? That counts as famous."

"Conner is just a hockey player. He isn't famous like Liam James! How do you not know who he is?" Nancy gawked at her.

"I don't know... I guess I don't listen to current music much."

"He is more than a musician. He is an icon, and he's here in Mystic Falls! This is the biggest thing to happen here that I can remember," she said nearly vibrating with excitement. "I mean, why was his bus even here?"

That was a fair point. Mystic Falls is an out of the way sleepy little town. It isn't really on the way to anywhere.

"Well, let's get the meeting room set up. I'm not sure what they will need, but let's set in some water, coffee, bagels and fruit. You know the drill," Lexi said, making her way to her office.

She looked over at Nancy, who was still standing at the front door on her phone.

"Nancy. We need to get the room set up. Also, we don't need to spread it around town that they are here, okay? Let's have some level of professionalism, please."

"Right," Nancy said with a sheepish grin on her face as she slid her phone back into her pocket. She stood there still as stone looking at Lexi.

"The meeting room?" said Lexi.

"Right!" She appeared to snap out of it and headed down the hall to start the set-up. Lexi would be irritated, but given she had just left her uneaten, unpaid for breakfast sitting on her table at Mae's in a similar situation, she really had no room for irritation.

She sat down at her desk and pulled up the availability to check just in case they all needed to stay overnight. Mystic Falls Inn was just a small town inn and could book up quickly. They only had twelve rooms and two cabins, but right now things were miraculously open.

If this had happened in the fall, they would be out of luck. That was high tourist season, but right now, in late June, things were more available. But hopefully they would have their bus up and running and they would be able to get back on the road. She went ahead and put a block on the rooms just in case.

Lexi stretched in her office chair. She still felt a vague fog from her earlier encounter. Coffee. She definitely needed coffee. She slipped away to pour herself some before the mass of people descended on the inn. As she filled up her cup, her phone vibrated in her pocket.

Poppy- LEXI! Is it true that Liam James is staying at the inn?

Small-town life. She would wager the whole town knew about all of this by now.

> Lexi- He's not staying here. Their bus broke down and it is getting repaired. They are using the meeting room today.

> Poppy- Hmmmm sounds like you guys could use a sandwich and baked goods delivery.

> Lexi- Well it's either that or ask Mark to stay on since we don't serve lunch.

> Poppy- Don't you dare. You take a lunch order, and I will bring them over personally. It is not something we usually offer, it would be special since you're such a valued customer.

> Lexi- Of course, this has nothing to do with you wanting to meet Liam James.

> Poppy- You wound me!

> Lexi- I will get back to you.

Taking a deep breath, Lexi tried to focus. This was going to be a long day; she could already feel it. Lexi was a creature of routine, and this morning was throwing her. As she made her way back to her office, her phone buzzed in her pocket again.

> Josh- Head's up. Poppy is going on about something with Liam James and the inn. I think she is going to text you.

> Lexi- Too late. I already told her if they
> need a lunch order I will be in touch.

Just as she was about to sit at her desk, she heard the front door open and a bunch of people come in. She stepped out into the reception area to greet them. It was the same as the diner, most of them on their phones all surrounding him.

"Is that meeting room available?" asked the woman who seemed to be in charge of this little circus.

"Yes, right this way," Lexi said, leading them down the hall into the meeting room that had been set up for them. As they all scuttled in and got out laptops and started to work, a hand settled on the small of her back. That touch sent a zing through her body like nothing she had ever experienced before. As she turned around, Liam's sudden presence sent shivers down her spine. She felt paralyzed, unable to move a muscle as he hovered behind her. The pull towards him, to be physically close to him, was like nothing she had ever felt before. No wonder he was a superstar.

"I was wondering if you might have any rooms available. I would love to take a shower," he said with his million-dollar smile. His eyes were kinder than Lexi would have imagined them to be, kind and deep brown. The dimples in his cheeks were so deep she just wanted to lick them. This was getting out of hand. She could not get wrapped up in all this nonsense.

"Of course. I'll go see which rooms are available and get a key for you."

"I'll come with you," said the woman.

"Perfect. You have the card for all of this?"

The woman gave her a face that said, 'you're stupid for even asking'.

"Right, well, follow me," said Lexi with her best service industry smile and voice.

They made their way back to the front desk and Lexi pulled up the computer to see what rooms were available. She put him in their best room, because he was a superstar after all, and turned to the back wall to get the key.

"What's this?" asked the woman looking at the key in her hand like it was a completely foreign object to her.

"That is the room key. I put him in eight. It has the best view in the inn. You can see the falls from the window."

"This is a room key?" She asked again.

"Yes. Can I please have your card to put on file for the rooms and other charges?" Lexi asked, struggling to keep the customer service smile on her face.

"Are you sure you don't need a piece of gold from my satchel?" the woman asked, still staring at the key in her hand like it was from another planet.

"I'm sorry?"

"I just haven't seen an actual room key before," she said, finally meeting Lexi's eyes.

"Yes, well, we are a little old school here, but we do need modern money."

"Right," said the woman, handing Lexi the card as she looked down at her phone screen.

Taking the black AmEx card from her hand, Lexi scanned it into her system.

"Do you think you might need more rooms tonight?" she asked.

"No, the bus should be up and running. We have a show tomorrow," she said curtly.

"Of course. If anything changes just let me know."

At that, the woman turned around without another word and left. Well, this was going to be an interesting day.

After taking care of the meeting room and other room, Lexi settled into as much of a normal schedule as she could. The front desk had been abandoned most of the morning. Nancy was busy taking excellent care of the water and coffee in the meeting room. Lexi decided just to let Nancy have her fun. It wasn't every day that their small town was visited by one of the country's biggest pop idols. But the work needed to be done, so Lexi settled herself behind the front desk, started getting today's check-ins ready, and finished the two check-outs they had that morning. It was a slow day today besides the famous distraction that was currently showering.

Woah. That was the wrong thought to have, but once that thought had taken hold, there was no shaking it. Lexi was just imagining him in the shower, water running down his chest, his soapy hands rubbing over his chest and arms and stomach and...

"Can I ask you a question?" She heard that velvety voice ask.

"Hmmm?" she almost purred, not looking up, still lost in her own thoughts. Her not safe for work thoughts.

"Those falls I could see from the window. Is there a trail to see those closer?"

She seemed to finally snap out of it only to be face to face in the empty reception area with Liam James. She could feel the flush creeping up her face.

"Oh yes, the falls. Sorry, yes. Those are the Mystic Falls. That is how the town got its name. Yes, at the back of our property here. There is a path that meets up with the nature park the falls are in, and that path will lead you right to the falls. It's an easy hike, just a little over a mile," she said.

"Maybe you could show me later," he said with that hypnotic smile on his face.

"I can have someone show you the path whenever you are ready," she said, trying to ignore the hundreds of butterflies fighting in her belly.

"But I want you to show me," he said. His eyes locked on hers as he reached out to take her hand. He was going to kiss her hand, and then Lexi would cease to exist; she would be nothing but a puddle on the floor.

"Liam, we need you in the meeting room."

Liam looked back at Lexi and cocked his eyebrow and gave her a wicked smile. "Maybe later then," he said as he turned to leave for the meeting room.

Lexi smiled as he walked away, feeling slightly dazed.

The woman standing in the doorway cleared her voice loudly. Lexi shook her head to try and combat the hypnotism this man seemed to have. She looked over at the woman standing in the archway of the reception area, arms crossed over her chest, and looking irritated.

"Is there anything I can help you with?" Lexi asked.

"No, we are good for now. But I just wanted to give you this list. It's how Liam likes to be interacted with by the staff."

"I'm sorry?"

"I know this is a small town, but we would appreciate your discretion and professionalism," she said with a biting edge to her voice.

"Of course," said Lexi, the customer service smile finding her face again. The woman handed her a piece of paper and Lexi took it. "While I have you here," she continued, "can I give you this menu? Just let us know what you would all like to order, and I'll take care of it for you."

The woman took it from her hand and turned and left.

Lexi looked down at the paper in her hand. It was a printed list of rules. She was already feeling a bit put off by the professionalism comment. Lexi was always a professional. Always.

As she made her way through the list, she realized how intense it was. The first couple things were fine, mostly about safety and security, no unauthorized pictures, no posting whereabouts on social media, things of that nature. Things her staff would never do, though she was going to check back in with Nancy anyway.

After that, the list got a bit weird. Apparently, there was to be absolutely no gluten. Fine, we all have allergies. Absolutely no pickles. Fine, we all have our food preferences. But no one could talk to Liam directly. If you needed to ask him a question, you needed to go through his manager. Anything Liam asked for needed to be okayed by his manager first. Any interaction with him would require an NDA. It didn't seem to make much sense. The rest of the list went over things like the thread counts and the square footage requirement of any room he stayed in. Lexi's head was reeling.

What did he think this was? A five-star resort? Luckily, they would not be staying the night because if his majesty needed this thread count, she would not be able to provide that. The inn only had one brand of sheets. And while they were nice sheets, nicer than any she had ever slept on, that's for sure, she was sure the thread count wasn't high enough.

Well, this list did the trick. It broke whatever spell she had been put under about dealing with his guy. She didn't know she was dealing with a privileged pompous ass, but she knew that now. Why did he talk to her at all if he wanted all communication from his manager? He had seemed decent enough, but apparently, he left the douchebaggery to his manager. She needed to call a staff meeting and ensure they were all on the same page with how to deal with these people. Of course, they would meet the demands she was able to. She was a goddamn professional, after all.

After she found Nancy, she gathered the rest of the staff to go over the finer points of the list. She didn't give them the whole list, just the highlights, but ever since that meeting, she had been in a foul mood. He had seemed... well, he had seemed almost like a god, but if this is the devotion he required, he was just an asshole. And really, should she be surprised? How had she let herself get swept up in his smile and charm?

It was getting into the afternoon, and she still hadn't heard if they were close to getting out of her inn.

Around lunchtime, Liam's manager came storming through the lobby. "Is this the only lunch in town?" the woman asked Lexi with the menu in her hand like it contained a flesh-eating virus.

"No, there are a few other restaurants. Is there anything in particular you are looking for? We have a great Italian Bistro."

"He can't eat gluten. Pasta is gluten."

"Right. That cafe menu does have gluten-free and vegan options, and they can work with most diet restrictions."

"Fine. Here is the order," she said, giving the menu to Lexi. The woman turned on her heel and walked back into the meeting room, shutting the door behind her.

The menu in her hand looked like it had been graded, and it had failed miserably. It was covered in writing. Each person's order had special instructions from diet restrictions to just plain preferences. Wow, a bunch of Hollywood types with eating a long list of diet restrictions, figures. Walking to the front desk, she picked up the phone and called Josh at the cafe. They had barely opened. She hoped they would be able to handle some of this stuff.

After a couple of rings, he picked up. "Hey Josh, Poppy said you guys might be able to handle a large lunch order."

"Yeah, what do you got?"

"I have a list from a bunch of Hollywood prima donnas with many unfortunate eating restrictions."

He chuckled into the phone. "Okay, I'll see what I can do. Do you want to give me the order?"

"I might just email you a picture of the menu, it's intense. And if you can get this for me, I'll owe you big."

"Of course, just send it over."

She took a picture of the menu and sent it to Josh. "You should be getting it soon."

"Yep, got it." He paused, "Wow... you weren't kidding."

"I know. I'm sorry, Josh." There was another pause while he read over the menu and the special orders.

"No, this should be doable. I'll send Poppy over with it when it is ready."

"Okay, but make sure she knows that she won't be able to meet him, and she shouldn't say on social media he is here. I probably shouldn't have even told you this order is for him. Liam James... I'm probably not even allowed to say his name out loud without his manager appearing to scold me and make me sign an NDA."

"What?" He was laughing on the other end of the line.

"Nothing, just tell Poppy he is secretive and all that."

"Gotcha. I'll talk to you later."

"Bye."

She returned the phone to the cradle, went to her office, and popped her earbuds in. Her plan was to do some mind-less computer work and lose herself in an audiobook. She needed a break from today.

About an hour later there was a knock at the door. Poppy poked her head in. "Hey Lexi, I have your order here. And Josh sent this one over for you," she said, taking out a white paper bag with her name on it.

"Perfect, thank you. I'll take these from you," she said as she stood to get the box.

"I really can't meet him?"

"I'm sorry, but no. He's very private."

"I understand, but a girl can dream." Lexi turned to Poppy and finally took her in. Her long dark hair was wet, and her shoulders were spattered with water.

"Is it raining?"

"Yeah, it kind of came out of nowhere. It was supposed to be clear, but it started raining on my way over, and it looks like it could be a pretty big storm," Poppy said. "I'm gonna get back to the cafe before this gets going," she said, gesturing to the nasty-looking rain clouds. "I'll talk to you later, Lexi."

"Bye," she said, following her out of her office with the box of lunch orders.

Making her way down the hallway to the meeting room, she situated the box so she could knock on the door.

"Come in," called a woman's voice behind the door.

Lexi managed to turn the handle and let herself in the room while carrying the box of orders. Liam stood to take the box from her. She hid her eyes, almost afraid to make eye contact. His hand grazed hers as she set it down, and there was that zing. Stupid zing. She just needed to get through this day, and all of these people, and that obnoxious zing, would be out of her hair.

She looked over to his manager. Her arms were once again crossed over her chest as she examined Lexi.

"Alright, lunch everyone," Liam said as he set out the bags.

"They included some apple cider donuts and some gluten-free muffins," said Lexi.

"We don't really eat carbs all that often," she said, giving Lexi a look she knew all too well. It was a look that said, 'I don't eat carbs, but it is clear you do'. Yes, Lexi was fat. She always had been, but she gave up letting it bother her many years ago. There were too many other things to worry about.

"Speak for yourself, Jacinda. I love carbs," she heard Liam say. Of course, his manager had a name like Jacinda. She turned to look at him as he took a bite of one of the apple cinnamon muffins. "Damn. These are perfect," he said to the muffin like it had just given him the biggest shock of his life.

"My sister-in-law makes them. She's the baker at the café."

"Nice," he said. She smiled at him; it was like she almost forgot he was a pretentious ass for a minute there.

A loud clap of thunder pulled her out of that moment. She looked over to his manager. "Thank you, we got it from here," she said with curt politeness.

"Okay, if you need anything else, just let me know," she said with a smile as she turned to leave.

As she passed the big bay window in the library, she could see it was really coming down. The wind had picked up, and the trees waved back and forth. She guessed she wouldn't be showing Liam the trail this afternoon. But it had been made clear that wasn't her place anyway. Hopefully, they would all clear out soon, and things would go back to normal. She closed her office door behind her and sank into her chair. Her eyes drifted to the bag in here with her name on it, and she was starving after leaving her breakfast uneaten on the diner table this morning.

She opened the bag and peeked inside. Bless her brother. In this bag was an apple cider donut, her favorite. A turkey BLT on fresh bread, her other favorite. And some type of Kale salad, not her favorite, but she would eat it, nonetheless.

Lexi- Thanks for lunch. What do I owe you?

Josh- You owe me a cookout. Friday. My house.

Lexi- Fine. See you then.

She unwrapped her sandwich and took one delicious bite. At that moment, the lightning flashed, and a crash of thunder shook the windows. Then the power went out.

Fuck.

She hung her head and waited for the knock at her door.

Chapter 4

Lexi

The loud knock came quickly. Lexi looked longingly at her sandwich and wrapped it back up. When she opened her door Jacinda stood there looking irritated.

"What happened?" she asked.

"It looks like the power went out."

"I know the power went out, stupid. But what are you doing about it?"

Woah. Lexi was no stranger to rude customers, but she would not allow herself to be abused like this.

"There is no reason for name-calling, I'm sure it will be back on soon. Just sit tight and I'll see what I can do."

"Don't you have any back-up generators or something? We can't work without wifi."

"I'm sorry, but that is not something we have, but I'll see what I can do," she said through her teeth.

"And we are expected to pay for a meeting room with no wifi? What kind of place is this?"

"Ma'am, I am not in charge of the weather. If you will

give me a moment, I can call the power company and find out how long we are supposed to be without power."

"Fine." She turned and left.

While no one would praise Lexi for her patience, she knew how to handle people, and she definitely knew how to handle her guests. But this woman was working her last nerve. She hadn't been talked to like this since last year when a mediocre Broadway actor named Damien St. Cloud stayed with them.

She picked up her phone and called the power company. There was a message about outages and that they were working as fast as they could to restore them, but that was all the information they had at the moment. That was not the information she wanted to pass on to that woman, but unfortunately, that is all they had.

"You have got to be fucking kidding me!" She heard someone yell in the reception area. Jumping up, she headed out to see what was the matter. "What do you mean the bus won't be ready today? Do you know who Liam James is? He has a sold-out concert tomorrow. A sold-out arena. You are just going to have to figure it out. I need to talk to your supervisor." There was a pause. "What do you mean you don't have a supervisor?" Then she pulled back and looked at her phone like it had just bitten her. "He hung up on me," she said to Lexi with a look of surprise on her face.

"Imagine that," said Lexi under her breath. "Are you going to need some rooms tonight?" Lexi asked with a phony smile.

"We.... may," she said with a grimace.

"Well, just let me know how many you need. Our chef will be back for dinner, and I'm sure we will be able to accommodate you."

"All of our bags are still on the bus," she said.

"I can get someone to drive the shuttle to get what you need from the bus."

"That might work. We'll need seven rooms."

"We have six available."

"Well, there are seven of us."

"Well, there are six rooms available."

This infuriating woman just stood there and looked at her like she would be able to pull more rooms magically out of her ass. And while Lexi's ass was quite sizable, she definitely wasn't storing extra inn rooms there.

"Could anyone share a room?" Lexi suggested, straining to remain polite. "Three of those rooms have two double beds."

"If we must."

"Okay, I'll get that all ready for you. Would you like someone to go with our driver to get what you need from the bus?"

"Yes. I'll send Cambria with him, so he doesn't mess anything up."

"Perfect. Cambria can meet him up here when she is ready."

And without another word, Jacinda turned on her heel and made her way out of the reception area.

"Charmer that one," said Nancy with a smile.

Turning to the front desk, Lexi found Nancy looking at her with wide eyes. "I know. She's a piece of work. Let's look at the two check-ins we have and start putting the Liam James people in rooms. I'll try and figure out what we can do with no power."

While Nancy took care of getting the Liam James people into their rooms, Lexi set to work trying to figure out what to do with no power. She called Mark, and he said he would be able to get a simple dinner together that would hopefully fit the eating restrictions of these people and his highness. Then she set to work to find all the candles in the inn. Eating by candlelight might be what they needed to do. She would also try to find as many flashlights as possible. This was a mess. She just wanted today to be over. Why did his stupid bus have to break down here? Where were they even going? Mystic Falls is off the beaten path.

The rain kept coming, it hadn't let up all day. Mark had come in looking like a drowned rat and gotten dinner off. Somehow, he managed to feed everyone. They had gotten everyone checked into their rooms, and things were winding down. Hiding from Jacinda had become a full-time job for Lexi. That woman was insufferable. Her watch read eight fifteen, and she was ready to get home for the day. Only there was one problem. She had left her damn car at the diner after being struck stupid by his Highness's smile. It was only eight blocks, and on a lovely sunny morning like this one was, it was an enjoyable walk. In the cold miserable rain... not so much.

She had a change of clothes here if she needed to stay, but they were sold out, and she didn't want to spend the night in her office. Hopefully the rain would let up soon and she could get back to her car. She knew she could text Josh if she needed to. In the past, she would have done it without thinking twice. But he was married now, and she was trying to not depend on him anymore. That meant she was on her own, and really she was fine with that. But for things like this, it would be nice to have someone to pick up the slack. Although, if she had a partner, she may not have fallen under the Liam James spell like she did and left her car at the diner.

It was closing in on eight thirty, and the rain was still pouring. She decided to sit on the inn's porch and see if she could brave the cold rainy walk back to her car. Walking out, she closed her eyes and listened to the steady fall of the rain. There was something about its steady but heavy rain that brought her peace. She took a deep breath and let the smell of rain and earth ground her. Finally, she was feeling her day fall away. She walked to the edge of the porch and put her hand out, and let the cold rain fall on it. Just then she was startled by the sound of an acoustic guitar playing on the other end of the porch.

Looking down she saw him. Liam James sat on the porch swing, still in his holey jeans and fitted white t-shirt. He had one foot up on the swing while he was draped across the rest, strumming his guitar, hair rumpled, looking like a fucking god. It was like a magazine cover came to life in front of her. Too bad he was an entitled prick with a list of ways to interact with the help.

"I'm sorry. I didn't see you there," she said as she turned to go back inside.

"Don't leave on my account. It looked like you were enjoying the rain as much as I am," he said in his smooth low voice.

She just stood there looking at him.

"Come sit," he said as he patted the swing next to him.

"I shouldn't. I should get back inside." Did he not remember his own rules? She wasn't allowed to talk to him. She should have to clear this conversation with his fucking manager.

He stayed right where he was strumming his guitar, and so did Lexi. She should go back inside, but she couldn't tear herself away.

"I love the rain. Sometimes life gets so busy. But every now and then nature just tells you to take it easy, whether you like it or not," he said to her in his easy manner. "We all need that reminder sometimes. To just slow the fuck down and enjoy the moment you're in."

Looking around Lexi realized she was now within reaching distance of the porch swing. He sat up a bit straighter and made room for her next to him. Was she really about to sit with Liam James on a porch swing in the rain? What even was her life right now? This may not be on the list of ways to interact with Mr. James, but he didn't seem to mind right now. So, Lexi sat.

The swing moved beneath her as Liam gently rocked them. They sat in silence for a while, enjoying the rain.

"Have you worked here long?" he asked.

"I've worked here in some capacity for almost twenty years. I started doing laundry here when I was fifteen and have worked probably every job, and now I'm the manager."

"Really? That's impressive."

Turning to look at him, her eyes big. "Really? My working at a small-town inn is impressive to a person like you?"

His eyes fell, and if Lexi wasn't mistaken, he looked almost hurt.

"A person like me?" he asked. "And what kind of person is that?"

"Ya know, a person who is used to this rich glamorous life. Staying in places much nicer than this, eating at fancy restaurants, gluten-free of course, not having to worry about money or having all these people working for you."

"Wow..."

"I apologize that didn't come out right," she said quickly, trying to remind herself to be a professional.

"No, I think it came out just the way you intended it to," he said, looking at her with a cocked eyebrow.

"What is that supposed to mean?"

"Nothing, I just get that a lot. People have all these preconceived notions of what my life must be like... but I hate to let you know, it's not what it seems to be."

"I'm sorry. It has been a long day. I meant no offense."

"It's okay. It's refreshing actually to have it said to my face. Usually, it is eye rolls and backhanded compliments," he said, looking away from her and starting the swing moving again.

"What do you mean refreshing?"

"Just sometimes I feel like people aren't always honest with me. So, I respect your honesty."

She looked down in her lap. She was suddenly feeling warm and self-conscious. She had to remind herself that this man was the same man with that ridiculous list. He probably had his staff drafting up an NDA right now with some porch swing in the rain clause. She felt a pull to this man, but she would wager millions of other people did, hence his superstar status. It didn't mean anything. They would be on the road tomorrow, and this would be nothing but an interesting story. But still, she remained on the porch swing. "But hey, Modern Times," he said.

What on earth did that mean? She turned to look at him to see if he would elaborate, but he was just there looking at her with this sweltering smile on his face.

"I'm sorry?" she asked.

His eyebrow cocked as he appeared to be waiting for her to say something, but she just looked at him. She didn't have the time for games with his highness.

"I just like a Lazy Sunday Morning much better than the Party Star."

What was even happening? Was he so unrelatable that he couldn't even have a conversation with someone as lowly as her?

"I mean, aren't we all Waiting for the Sun to Shine?" he asked with a completely unreadable look on his face.

"It's past eight. I don't think the sun is going to shine anymore," she said, unsure of what else to say.

"Midnight Groove," he looked at her astounded.

"Are you having some sort of episode? Because I will definitely have to sign an NDA then," she said that last part under her breath.

He looked at her, the only light from the fireplace on the other side of the window, but she could see the hint of a smile and a look in his eyes that she couldn't quite read. She smiled back at him because she couldn't help it. She was drawn to him. He put his hand on top of hers that was resting on the swing between them. The heat of his palm on the back of her hand sent shivers through her. She had never felt this way before. A spark danced between them, and her lips parted as she took a sharp intake of air.

He moved his face closer to hers, and his thumb caressed the side of her hand. She was going to burst into flames right here. What was even happening? Because she would swear she was about to be kissed, but that didn't make any sense. It made even less sense than the words he had been spewing at her.

"Are you okay?" she asked, embarrassed by how breathless and needy she sounded.

"I think I'll manage." Leaning even closer to her, he picked up the hand that had been resting on hers. The sudden chill on her hand had her itching to reclaim it. But then he raised that same hand to her face, tucked a stray lock of hair behind her ear, and ran the backside of his finger down her cheek and along her soft jawline. Her entire body was on fire. She wanted him to kiss her. It was verging on need. This urgent feeling was totally foreign to her. She needed him to close the distance, that at some point had become a matter of inches and claim her mouth. Her lips parted as her body thrummed with excitement. He gave her a delicious smile and slowly licked his bottom lip as he closed the distance between them.

At that moment, the porch light and the light inside the window turned on, shining its harsh light on their soft intimate moment. Reality plummeted towards her as she squinted at him. He gave a soft chuckle but didn't move away.

The sound of someone clearing their voice harshly by the door pulled their focus. There standing at the door, looking extremely annoyed, was his damn manager.

"We've had a development," she said, "you're needed inside."

"Right." He stood and turned back to Lexi. "It was lovely chatting with you. I look forward to our next meeting." His mouth turned into that smile of his as he winked at her. She didn't respond. Her brain was still frozen trying to figure out what had just happened.

He turned to walk back in. Jacinda did not follow him in but was standing there glaring at her.

"Well, it looks like the power is back on," Lexi said to her with a forced smile.

"What was that about?" she asked, ignoring Lexi's attempt to lighten the situation.

"That? That was nothing. We just bumped into each other out here." Jacinda just continued to glare. Rage and embarrassment were building inside of Lexi, and if she did not remove herself from this situation right now that rage would bubble over. "If you'll excuse me, I'm getting ready to leave."

Lexi walked right past her and into the inn.

"You'll have an NDA on your desk in the morning."

She couldn't be serious. "I'm sorry, whatever for?"

"You read his list," the woman stated back plainly and headed up the stairs.

Lexi made her way to her office and slammed her door. She needed to get out of this inn. She grabbed her purse and rummaged through a bin until she found one of those plastic ponchos the inn kept for guests and decided to walk back to her car. It was still pouring down rain, but she didn't care. She needed to get out of this place.

Chapter 5

Liam

Liam went to his room and waited for Jacinda. Even though today didn't go according to plan, he felt more alive than he had in a long time. Something about this place and the beautiful woman on the porch spoke to him. There was something here. He just wasn't sure what, but this was the most inspiration he had felt in almost a year.

He knew that she was a bad idea. The decision not to get involved with anyone after everything with Henry was a decision he was sticking to. His life was too crazy. He should just put this all out of his mind and get back to the schedule.

Before he was Liam James, he had grown up in a town a little bigger than this one. That was when he was still just Liam Sheffield. He loved being Liam James now. He loved the community he was able to give his fans, he loved creating music, but sometimes it was lonely.

He was supposed to be in the next city getting ready for the concert tomorrow night. After a day of meetings that resolved nothing, that should be his focus. But he still couldn't get this wonderful woman off his mind. And after that interaction, he knew she wouldn't be leaving his thoughts any time soon.

He had been sure she was a fan by how she got flustered around him, but when he started naming his song titles, she looked at him like he was from another planet. He wouldn't be conceited to say most of the country knew a couple of his bigger hits. He had just performed Modern Times on SNL a month ago. That song and Midnight Groove were both sitting at the top of the Billboard charts right now and had been for over a month. If she were a fan, she would have known them, and not looked at him like he had lost his mind. This woman was growing more intriguing by the minute. She had seemed to be flustered by him but not because of his stardom. That was not something he had encountered before.

And if the lights hadn't come back on, he would have kissed her. And fuck... he wanted to kiss her. He wanted to do a whole lot more than kiss her, but he wasn't sure what all that meant yet. And he wanted to be sure. His life was not his own, and his image was complicated. He had survived a rough couple of years when the media had gotten wind of his relationship with his touring bassist.

Those around him knew he was bisexual. He was kind of the poster boy for positive masculinity which made many people question his sexuality in inappropriate ways. He didn't care if people knew he was bisexual and refused to hide it. But his sexuality and who he was attracted to made no difference in the art he created, and he refused to let that be the story. His shows were a place for people to just exist and be themselves regardless of who they were and if society accepted them.

One particular song called Home was hard for him to

sing every night because it spoke of finding a home and a family where you feel love, which isn't always your own. The tears that would stream down the faces of some of his fans at that song gutted him. If he could give them a night and a safe place to be who they are, then all the strain and bullshit of this line of work was worth it. He could handle it, but he wouldn't put anyone else through it, especially anyone he cared about. Being involved with him just came with too high a cost.

He sat on his bed kicking his feet up and waited for Jacinda to come. This was a nice little inn, and the view from his room was wonderful. He had to see those falls before he left town.

There was a soft knock at his door. "Come in," he called.

Jacinda entered looking irritated. She was irritated most days, but this day had been one for the books from start to finish.

"So, I just received an email. The arena you were supposed to perform at tomorrow night got hit by this storm. Apparently, the roof took some damage and there was extensive flooding, so we're going to have to cancel the show."

"What do you mean cancel the show?" He hated that. He loved his fans, and he knew many of them saved up and came from far away to see his shows. "We're going to reschedule and offer full refunds if they can't make the new date. It's all being worked out."

"Can we do something on social media? Maybe a private online show for ticket holders as an apology?"

"I'll see what we can put together. It would take a bit of the pressure off. Our next date is in five days in New York. I can get you airlifted out of here tomorrow and get you home for a few days."

He nodded along as she rattled off a few other things, but he was looking out the window. Though it was dark, and he could no longer see the falls, he knew they were there. He wanted to explore them. He wanted to explore this town. He wanted to explore that intriguing woman behind the front desk, but he would keep that one to himself.

"Why don't we hold off on the airlift or whatever. We can wait here. This might be a nice little change of pace for us. The paparazzi aren't here, and this might be a good place to shoot the Home video."

She scrutinized him for a long moment. "This wouldn't have anything to do with whatever I interrupted on the porch?"

He narrowed his gaze. "No, it doesn't. And quite frankly, that is none of your business."

"Liam," she cocked her head to the side and looked at him with her own version of loving eyes. "Everything you do is my business. I am just trying to avoid another scandal."

"Still, why don't we stay and do some location scouting? This place could be perfect."

"Fine, we'll deal with the rest of this in the morning," she said, irritation dripping with every word.

"You are a charmer, Jacinda." He smiled at her. His prickly manager had taken some getting used to. She ran a tight ship, but he was kind of a pushover, so he guessed it was for the best.

"Good night, Liam," she said as she left, closing the door behind her.

He laid back on his bed and pulled his guitar over him. It was his own version of a security blanket. This guitar had gotten him through some tough times. He absent-mindedly strummed some chords, thinking about Lexi. He wondered what that was short for. Alexis? Alexandra? Maybe it was just Lexi. He would find out. His mind replayed that moment on the swing, the softness of her face as he caressed it. The way her lips parted with a sharp inhale of breath. She felt it too. But if she wasn't a fan, then maybe it was just him, and not what his stardom had to offer. The thought settled deep inside of him. He needed to know more.

Chapter 6

Lexi

By the time Lexi had gotten to her car last night she was soaked to the bone. She managed to get home, but she was still trying to recover from her tumultuous day. Part of her wished they had left. She wasn't sure if she could handle another day like that, but a part of her couldn't stop thinking about that man. How was it when she was with him, she almost forgot about that list and who he was?

When she got home, she decided to google Liam James. There were so many hits and articles and pictures of his beautiful face. There were some pictures of him on stage performing for a big outdoor festival that stuck out to her. He was wearing a dress shirt with a pink sequined vest with black tattoos peeking out of the open buttons. She saw another of his smiling face on a magazine cover with those dimples you could damn near swim in. Then, one of him sitting in a field somewhere with his guitar, looking rugged and masculine, except for the pearl necklace and painted fingernails. Lexi couldn't stop looking at him.

But some scandals seemed to be following him. At that,

Lexi closed her computer. She didn't want to know. She wasn't sure why, but it felt like an invasion of privacy. He was a real person, not some item for tabloid fodder. She had never really been one to pay too much attention to that kind of stuff.

As she walked into the inn the following morning, she stopped and looked over at the porch swing. It was there just as it always was. It showed no sign of the conversation that had happened there last night, of the almost kiss that danced between her and Liam. It was unbelievable. Lexi couldn't believe she had almost kissed a pop star on the inn's front porch last night. It was unbelievable for many reasons. For one, she definitely shouldn't be kissing guests at work, but in what world does she kiss people like Liam James? Those types of things didn't happen to her. She had almost convinced herself that it all would have been a dream when she opened the door and walked in. That made more sense than it being a reality.

Opening the door, the inn was crowded. It would appear the entire staff had shown up. This was ridiculous. She would need to check to see who actually was supposed to be here and send the rest of them home.

"Hey Lexi, Liam's manager was looking for you," said Nancy as she was organizing today's check-ins.

"Did she happen to say what she needed?" Lexi was not looking forward to talking to that insufferable woman.

"Nope. I'm sure she'll find you though," Nancy said with a smirk.

"I'm sure she will. And can you find out who is actually on the schedule? It would seem our whole staff decided to come in to work today."

"Are you surprised? Nothing this exciting has ever

happened in Mystic Falls before," said Nancy with an amused look on her face.

"Yes, but people who aren't on the schedule need to go home."

"I'll figure it out," Nancy said with a sigh.

"Thank you." Lexi went into her office and shut the door. She had a feeling it was going to be another long day. One that required more coffee than she'd had. Instead of getting more coffee, she opened her laptop and searched his name again, just to look at him.

Once Nancy found out who needed to be there today, Lexi made the rounds sending everyone home. People didn't seem very happy with her, but she was the boss; it wasn't her job to make people happy.

Stopping for her third cup of coffee, she talked to Mark.

"I haven't found out when they are all leaving, but would you be able to do a lunch, or should I talk to Josh again to get them an order ready."

"I think I should be able to put something together, but the diet restrictions are tough. I mean, I think there has to be a gluten-free option, a vegan option, a paleo option. When did people stop just eating food?"

"I know. Hopefully they will be out of here today. Let's hope their bus is fixed."

With that she made her way back to her office. Her emotions were so jumbled up. She was still trying to piece together the guy she had sat on the swing with and the guy who needed an NDA to talk to. It was almost like he was two completely different people. Her life had been the same every day for so long. This was not the kind of disruption she was used to, and she was ready for it to be over.

A firm knock shook the door. Lexi closed her eyes and braced herself for what fresh hell was on the other side.

"Come in," she called.

The door opened to find Jacinda on the other side, looking irritated as ever.

"Oh good, you are finally in. It looks like we are going to be staying for a few more days. I just wanted to let you know."

"I will check to see what we have available," said Lexi. She knew there was availability, but she wished there wasn't. "Is your bus not fixed yet?"

"I actually haven't heard yet, but Liam's next show was canceled, and he would like to stay here and scout some spots for his next video. He apparently thinks this place has... charm," she said, looking around with a general disgust. "I don't see it, but it's not my vision."

"Well, I'll get you all booked. Let me know if you need anything else."

"That will be it for now. I will be in contact about last night."

"What about last night?"

"Don't give me that. The little stunt you pulled on the porch. You may be a fan, but it is incredibly unprofessional to try and get close to him while he's staying at your place of employment," Jacinda said coolly.

"I merely ran into him on the porch. He invited me to sit with him. That was it."

"We'll see, I will be talking to him later today."

At that she turned and left Lexi's office. Lexi grabbed the stapler off her desk with every intention of heaving it at the door closing behind her, but she just squeezed it and firmly set it down on her desk and took a deep breath. She could do this. She had gotten through worse things in her life. Dealing with a pompous privileged pop star would not get to her. Deep breath in for three, out for three.

She got them all booked into their rooms for the next couple of days. She needed to go inform Mark and the kitchen staff of the change.

"Hey, Mark," she walked into the kitchen. This time of day, the kitchen was generally slowing down from the breakfast rush and starting to wrap up until it would be time for dinner. "It looks like Liam James and his people will be staying with us for a few more days."

"Well, that just fucking great isn't it," he said, tossing an empty mixing bowl into the sink with a loud clank.

"I sense trouble," Lexi said tentatively.

"His manager just left," Mark continued getting angrier and angrier by the minute. "Checking everything and going over our ingredients and procedures to make sure they would be up to his standards. He didn't even come down for breakfast, which is fine by me, but he cannot just send his people into my kitchen to inspect my staff and my ingredients. We only have the freshest ingredients. No, we don't have tofu, tofu wasn't on the menu, but apparently, it is now. No gluten, no preservatives, no food dye, the last two have never been in my kitchen! I get allergies, but I swear that woman was getting joy out of being a pain in my ass."

Lexi sighed and poured herself a cup of coffee. "I'll talk to her and see if I have any more luck, but I'm not certain I will."

She turned and left, her thoughts on the list she had been given. This whole thing was getting out of hand. She could put up with it for a day, but her nerves were already shot, and it wasn't even lunchtime.

As she rounded the corner to the front desk, she saw Nancy with an apologetic look on her face.

"Oh, for fucks sake, what is it now?" Swearing in the lobby before ten, it was just apparently that kind of a day.

Nancy pulled out a manilla envelope and handed it to Lexi. "She brought this down for you." Nancy offered her an encouraging but pathetic smile. Lexi closed her eyes. In for three, out for three. She opened her eyes and took the envelope and turned and headed into her office.

She sat at her desk and opened the envelope. She pulled out a bunch of papers stapled together and right there across the top was written Nondisclosure Agreement. Were these people serious? She had one interaction with this man on the porch and now she was going to have to sign an NDA? This was nonsense. She was going to scream... or cry... or scream and cry. Either way, she needed to get out of there. She slammed the paper down on her desk and stood and walked out.

"Nancy. I'm taking a walk. Don't need me. I'll be back soon."

"You got it."

Lexi walked out the front door and down the stairs. She took a deep breath as she felt the tears pooling in her eyes. Picking up the pace, she turned the corner, desperate to find a place to collect herself.

Chapter 7

Liam

Liam awoke from one of the best night's sleep he'd had in a while. Sleep had been something that eluded him more and more. It seemed the more his creativity was blocked the worse his sleep got. Feeling more rested than normal, he was ready to get out and explore this town and that waterfall. There was something special here, he could feel it. There was a soft knock at the door.

"Come in," he called. In came Jacinda carrying a breakfast tray.

"Are you room service?" he asked.

"No. I just don't trust these people," she said with a sense of disgust.

"I think they are perfectly trustworthy," he said.

"Well, nonetheless, here is your breakfast." She sat it down at the table in the corner of the room. Taking the lid off he saw an omelet that looked good. Taking a bite, holy crap. It was really good.

"This is really good. The food here has been great."

Jacinda just stood there shaking her head.

"Okay, Liam. What is the agenda for the day? I know

you wanted to do some location scouting. I can find out if we can get a tour guide to show us around. I think that would be the most efficient use of our time. Then maybe we can get out of here tomorrow, back to civilization. There isn't even a Starbucks in this town."

"I don't need a tour guide. I can look around just fine, and I grew up in a town just a little larger than this. I think it's charming."

"It's something alright," she said under her breath.

"Did we get anything set up for the fans who are missing the concert tonight?"

"Yes, they were all sent a code to enter, you just have to log in and stream it. It should be pretty straightforward."

"Perfect. I'll work up a small acoustic set for the night and find the best place to film."

"I thought we could just do it in the meeting room here. Set up the lighting and a stool and you can do your thing."

He nodded thinking about logistics. "That could work. I'll let you know later."

He finished up his breakfast ignoring his manager. He was looking forward to getting out there, and he knew where he was headed first. As he sat eating his breakfast, he looked out his window at the falls in the distance. It was a beautiful sunny day out there and he was going to go and find those falls. That was at the top of the list.

Jacinda finally left his room, and he was happy for the reprieve. If he was being honest with himself, he could really use a break from her too. He could use a break from all of this. He would go live tonight for his fans, but then he had a couple days of nothing. He was supposed to be spending those in the city, but that wouldn't be relaxing. This town would be a place he could actually relax, and he was excited for that. There was something about this town that already felt like home. And while that shouldn't be possible, Liam wanted to trust his instincts, and they were telling him there was something special here. He was a little out of practice at trusting himself, but the pull to this place... and to Lexi, if he was honest, was more intense than anything he had felt in recent history.

After Jacinda left, Liam decided to sneak out. She normally insisted on knowing his whereabouts, but she could get over it. He needed some peace. Slipping on his shoes, he grabbed his room key and phone and headed out the door. Yesterday Lexi had told him there was a trail at the back of the inn that would lead to those falls, and he was going to find it.

As he walked along the back of the property, he found the trail and started down it. It was beautiful. The trees turned into a canopy above him, and all the noise faded away except for the birds overhead. The trail right now was a well-manicured path covered in wood chips. Yesterday's rain had made things muddy, but manageable. He wondered what the trail might be like further down.

As he walked down the path, the river came into view, he was on the bluff above. It was beautiful to look at. He continued to walk until he saw a bench in the distance. On the bench was a familiar figure. He was almost certain it was Lexi.

Something inside him lit up at the prospect of another meeting with her. He had come close to kissing her last night, and it had been a while since he had kissed anyone. He'd been having a hard time getting close to people recently, which wasn't like him. He was a people person. He made connections easily. It was part of his charm. Maybe it was just fame, but it all felt a bit much these days.

But there she was on the bench. Something in his heart

stirred, and he wanted to be close to her. He needed to be close to her. He wasn't sure why, but he did. This was probably a bad idea. It couldn't be anything but a good time. Being Liam James was an all-encompassing job, and sometimes he lost track of who he was. He couldn't be a good partner to anyone like that.

But that didn't seem to stop him because here he was, making his way over to the bench. He kept waiting for her to hear him coming, not wanting to surprise her or scare her, but he was getting really close now. In another step, he would be able to reach out and touch her. He cleared his throat to announce his presence and she jumped. Then as she turned, her hands were wiping at her eyes which were glassy and red. She was crying. Why was she crying? He needed to make it right. Right now.

"Are you okay?" he asked.

Smiling up at him with a smile he would recognize as fake from a mile away, she wiped away another tear. "I'm great. I should probably head back in."

"Don't leave on my account. I've been told I'm a pretty good listener if you want to talk."

She scoffed and rolled her eyes. He would be a little offended if he weren't concerned about her.

"Can I sit?" He asked tentatively, waiting for her answer.

"Sure, I mean, why sign one NDA when I can sign two?" She said dryly, but still scooted over, offering him a seat.

An NDA? What was she talking about?

"What do you mean?" He asked, lost.

"Don't worry, I'll sign it. I just needed to clear my head before I could read all the legal jargon and find out exactly what I am agreeing to," she said, sounding defeated and staring down at the flowing water beneath the bluff.

"I'm not following you, Lexi."

She turned to look at him, eyes squinted trying to parse his meaning.

"The NDA that is currently sitting on my desk," she said, irritation starting to creep in.

"What NDA? What are you talking about?"

"Because of last night, you invited me to sit with you and it broke one of the precious rules."

"What? What rules? Lexi, I am at a total loss about what the fuck is going on?" He was starting to get irritated too.

"The list," she said as she started ticking her fingers. "Thou shalt not serve his highness gluten. Thou shalt not take any pictures at threat of a long painful death. Thou shalt not speak to him without first surviving the quest of the manager."

He couldn't help but laugh. Did she just call 'him his highness'? No one had been this real with him in months, and he loved it.

"Well excuse me for having celiac disease," he said with a grin.

"I have to go back to work." She stood up from the bench quickly and turned to leave.

Liam reached out and grabbed her hand. There it was again, that zing that he felt every time he touched her. What was that? They both just stopped for a moment and looked at their hands, frozen in time. But he needed to get to the bottom of this list, because he knew zero fucks about what she was talking about.

"I'm serious though, Lexi. What list?"

"You're serious?" she asked seemingly taken aback by that knowledge.

"I am. I'm not sure what list you're talking about."

"Your manager. She gave me a list of things people needed to know to interact with you."

His eyebrows drew together, and a scowl found his face. "I'm sorry, what now?"

"I mean the first couple were totally fine, the gluten thing, obviously that's fine. No pictures. No posting your whereabouts on social media. I get all of that, but some of the other ones are intense..." She stopped and looked at him and cocked her head. "Do you really not know about this?"

"Not a damn thing." He could feel the anger seeping in. Jacinda. That was the only answer. She was controlling, but he never dreamed she would go this far. "What NDA are you talking about?"

"Last night... on the porch. The list said any unapproved contact with you will involve signing an NDA... You really know nothing about this?" He shook his head but held her gaze. "Well, this morning your manager put an NDA on my desk. It was just kind of the last straw; you know what I mean? My staff is bending over backward trying to help you all in any way we can, and we are happy to do it, but it has just been a lot. Your manager went into the kitchen and looked at all the ingredients and recipes and questioned the staff. I had to talk my chef down because he is not used to that."

"Of course, he's not. I apologize. My stay here has been wonderful. I'll apologize to your chef myself if that would help. And do not sign that NDA. It is unnecessary. I'll get to the bottom of this."

He put his hand on hers again and brought her back down onto the bench next to him.

"Can you tell me more about this list and what has been going on? I clearly need to make it known to Jacinda what is within her job parameters."

She was still for a moment just looking at her hand in his. The pull he felt toward her was something he had never experienced before.

"I don't want to get anyone in trouble..." she said quietly, still looking at their hands.

"Hey," he put his hand on her chin and gently lifted her head so she was looking at him. Big mistake. That was a big mistake because all he wanted to do was kiss her, but he wouldn't do that until all of this was taken care of. "You did nothing wrong. Don't sign that NDA and I will have a talk with my manager. If my staying here has caused you this level of stress," he said carefully wiping away the last tear that had escaped from her eye, "then corrections need to be made, and I'll handle them. Would you like me to leave? I know dropping my... presence... on a small place like this unexpectedly is a lot. I should've been more thoughtful. I'm just really enjoying your little town. It reminds me of home."

"It reminds you of home? How can that be?"

He chuckled. "I haven't always been a celebrity. I grew up in a small town not too much bigger than this one in Ohio."

"Did you really?" She asked, eyes a little brighter, their hands still clasped. He slowly started to rub her hand with his thumb.

"When I first met you at the diner, I thought you were a fan, but I'm beginning to think that might not be the case."

"I recognized you in the diner. Like clearly you were a celebrity, and you looked familiar, but I couldn't quite place you. I'm sorry."

"Don't be sorry. I like that. No wonder when I mentioned some of my more popular songs last night you looked at me like I was crazy," he said with a soft smile.

"Ohhh. That makes more sense, I thought you were having a stroke or were just so out of touch with the common man you forgot how to converse with us lowly peasants," she said with a laugh.

He couldn't help it, he laughed. He laughed out loud, and it felt good. No one besides his family and close friends had given him shit like that in so long. It was refreshing to be around.

"I like your honesty. You'd be surprised how many people around me tell me only what I want to hear. It's like they're scared of me."

"You're not so scary," she said with a smile. Though they'd had a number of interactions before, this was the first time he saw her genuine smile. Not her professional smile, but a smile that actually matched the way she felt on the inside and it was everything. He wanted to kiss her. He wanted to do so much more, but he needed to take care of this NDA and whatever was going on with Jacinda before he could even think about acting on that. Okay, well he would think about acting on it, because how could he not. Bad idea? ... quite possibly, but he was caring less and less.

"Thank you, I don't think I'm all that scary either," he said with a smile. "Now I had planned on hiking to the falls, but I think that has to wait. I'm going to go talk with Jacinda. Would you mind giving me the list that she gave you? I'm interested to see what my demands are, since I'm not even sure myself."

He stood and helped her up by the hand he was still holding.

"I can't believe you knew nothing about the list," she said with disbelief. "I wondered why you seemed like two different people, the person I had that moment with on the porch swing and His Royal Highness of the Ridiculous List." She chuckled to herself.

The next moment her eyes flew to his and she snatched back her hand. Liam could see a flush moving up her chest to her cheeks. Was she blushing?

"What's up?" He asked her clearly amused by her sudden bashfulness. He liked that she spoke her mind, but he did like this too.

"What? Oh, it's nothing. I mean, I didn't mean to insinuate we had a moment on the swing. It was just two people talking, one of us normally and the other one cryptically in his own song titles," she said, her voice dripping with sarcasm.

He laughed at her again. "Oh, there was definitely a moment. And after I take care of all of this, maybe I can take you out for dinner and we can create another moment just as nice as that one."

She stopped in her tracks. "Are you serious?"

"I am, unless you're going to reject me... in that case, it was just a joke."

"You're asking me out?" her brow was drawn, and she was studying him.

"I am. I have an online concert to do tonight for the fans that had the venue rescheduled, but after that, if you're free?"

"You, Liam James, are asking me out?" She asked incredulously as she gestured to her body, as if he wasn't aware he was asking her out. He was aware, he was very aware.

He gave her a slow smile and cocked his eyebrow and nodded. "I sure as fuck am. And you haven't answered me yet. Don't leave me hanging."

"Yeah, I guess I could do that." She bit her bottom lip and looked up at him through her lashes. Liam fought hard against all his baser instincts screaming at him to pull her to him and claim her mouth. Although if he was being honest, there was a part of him that was scared, because if she felt as good as he thought she would, he would never want to let go.

"Good. Now can you please show me this list?"

"Of course, follow me," she said, her professional voice setting back in. He was interested in knowing all her voices.

He followed her back up to the inn and into her office. As they walked by the front desk clerk, he smiled at her and she froze, dropping her stapler. It clattered to the floor with a loud clunk. "Oh goodness," she squeaked as she disappeared behind the desk to retrieve the stapler.

He followed Lexi into her office. It was a small space with blue walls with some certifications hung up. Nothing to give him any hint into who she was as a person, and he was hungry for any morsel that would help to give insight into the woman sitting at the desk before him. The half-full coffee mug on her desk read 'cup of ambition.' He liked a good Dolly Parton reference, but he wanted more.

A-ha! A framed picture on the desk. Surely, she wouldn't mind if he picked it up and snuck a look at what was so important it was the only picture on her desk. But when he looked at it, he wished he hadn't. It was Lexi with this tall, boy next door type, with a smile that let you know that he was an amazing person. No morally gray choices there. Nope, just golden retriever energy all the way. Of course, that is the kind of guy who she was with. The thought made him recoil with anger, he wasn't sure why, but it was sure there. Jealousy. Fucking jealousy.

He looked back down at her. She was sitting there holding a manilla envelope smiling at him. "That's my brother," she said.

"I'm sorry?" He wasn't following her, his brain had been pinging from the photo to the NDA in her hands and the assistant he needed to talk to, none of them felt very good. But then it hit him what she had said.

"The photo, that's me and my brother."

"Oh good. No reason to be jealous then," he said with a smile.

"Jealous? Why on earth would you be jealous?" She said, baffled.

"Because if an attractive man is going to have his arm around you, I would prefer it to be me."

Her mouth fell open and her eyes widened. And he had the urge to sweep everything off this desk and take her right here... well, that escalated quickly.

She took a moment to gather herself. "Unless I was dreaming, you did ask me out back there, right? If I had a boyfriend, then it would be pretty shitty of me to say yes."

"Nope, you're right. You are never what I expect."

"I could say the same about you," she said with a small smirk.

"So, is that the NDA?" He asked, pointing to the envelope in her hands.

"Yes, I can still sign it. Like I said, I just needed to clear my mind before I tried to understand legal speak."

"I assure you, that isn't necessary. And the list you say exists?"

"Right," she said as she opened her top desk drawer and gave him the paper.

He examined it. What in the hell was this? No wonder he had been so isolated recently. The first few were reasonable and important, but as the list went on it made him seem like he was this pompous douchebag. No wonder no one looked him in the eye anymore. Her calling him his highness made total sense after seeing this list.

"What's going on here?" he heard a familiar voice ask. Jacinda.

"I was just having a conversation with Lexi here," he said, trying to mask some of the anger that was rolling through him.

She looked at him, the envelope in his hand, then to the list in the other. Her eyes went wide, and she shot a look over at Lexi.

"You told on me?" She snapped with annoyance like they were fighting siblings, not like they were the professionals he had assumed them both to be.

"This has nothing to do with her. We need to have a talk, Jacinda, about exactly what your role is here. Follow me." He turned to leave without turning back to Lexi. He would have time to talk to her later and smooth all this over. Right now, Jacinda had some big explaining to do.

He walked up the stairs to his room and dug into his pocket for the key to unlock the door. She followed behind him. When they got in, he handed her the list of his supposed demands. "Care to explain?" He opened the envelope pulling out the NDA. It seemed to be a fairly standard issue NDA, but what business did she have issuing NDAs on his behalf?

"You have no idea the behind-the-scenes work that goes into doing this, so you can just sit there and strum your guitar and bat your eyelashes," she spat at him.

Well, that didn't go how he was expecting.

"My guitar strumming and eyelash batting, as you so fucking nicely put it, is what pays your paycheck, and the paycheck of everyone here. Try that again."

"I'm sorry. I just do this so things go smoother. It just makes sense to get these things out of the way."

"Yes, some of these things make sense. The first five are great. Let's keep those, but the rest have to go. And right now, with the disrespect and going behind my back, I think you have to go too."

She gasped. "Are you firing me?"

"I don't know... maybe. I need some time to cool down." He raked his hand through his hair. He needed to calm down. No wonder Lexi had been so upset. The thought that she was upset because of Jacinda made him want to fire her and not look back. That couldn't be the reason, but all of this could.

He plopped down in the chair by his window and looked out at the falls he had hoped to hike to. But apparently, he was dealing with this shitstorm instead.

"Here's what we are going to do. You are leaving--" he said.

"You can't do that! Please, let's talk about this," she begged.

"No. I just need some space. There's a lot on my mind. Right now, you are going to make sure everything is set up for the streaming event tonight. I'll talk to Lexi to make sure we can have the room and film there. After that, you and the whole team are going to leave."

"Leave? What do you mean leave?" She asked gawking at him.

"I'm calling the car service and sending cars for you and everyone else. I'll remain here until the next concert date. When I need to be there, I will be, but until then I'm here. On my own."

"You can't be serious! Just leave you here by yourself?"

"I'm a grown man. I've survived on my own for years, I think I can manage."

"My father will not be happy about this. I can't just leave you."

He looked at her. Her father? What did he have to do with any of this? Yes, he was on his legal team, but he had no say on who Liam hired as his manager.

"Well, this is what is happening. Pack your bags. Set up the meeting room and I'll call cars for everyone."

"No, it's fine. Let's just figure this out. We can scout today and then get back to the city."

"Jacinda, if you do not get out of this room right now you are fired. I'm trying to calm down here, there is still a big fucking chance you are fired anyway. So, I would stop pushing it and leave. Now."

She turned and left, the door shutting behind her. Liam raked his hand down his face. What the hell just happened? He didn't like the way she was treating people. And the way she had acted like he didn't have the right to fire his own fucking manager just pissed him off. He felt like there was something he was missing because that entire situation seemed fucked.

A shower. He needed a shower, but first things first. He called up his car service and ordered cars to take everyone back to the city. Then he headed into his bathroom and turned on the shower to just about scalding. He needed to clear his mind before his show. And his date.

Chapter 8

Lexi

As Liam and Jacinda left the office Lexi laid her head on her desk with a thud. What the hell had just happened? Had she just been asked out by a pop star she thought was a pompous douchebag, only to find out he knew nothing about all the douchebag things he had done? Not that he had been a douchebag to her, because it was quite the opposite in fact. He had been lovely. Every encounter they had was lovely. She just thought he was a douchebag because of that fucking list, and it turns out he didn't know anything about it.

Not only that, but she felt this magnetic pull whenever he was around. Is it possible he felt it too? He seemed to, at least a little bit, but what on earth would they have in common? He dated movie stars and models, not people like Lexi.

Sure, physically she didn't think she was his type, but her life was also boring. She loved her boring life. Yes, she should see her brother more and she could get out of the house a little more, but she was happy here at her job and she was content to go home and live her life.

She was, wasn't she?

She had never really thought about it before because what was the point? Her job paid the bills and that was fine. When she really stopped to think about it, what could she have in common with him? All she knew was this inn. She had given up so much when she was younger and life was about survival. She didn't even know who she was outside of that.

But that was a problem for another day. Today she was going out tonight with Liam James. She was tempted to google him again, find out more, but she knew she had things about herself she would want to reveal in her own time, and who was she to take that decision away from him? Suddenly her phone was dinging on her desk.

Poppy- Hey Lexi, just seeing if you needed a lunch order today.

Lexi- Let me check, I'll get back to you.

She left her office, and Nancy was on the phone. "Yes Sir, I will get everyone checked out right away. If you need anything else, just let me know." Then she put the phone back in its cradle.

"What's that all about?" Lexi asked.

"Well, that was Liam James. Apparently, they are all checking out today." Lexi's heart sank. Of course, she was just being foolish. Of course, he was going back to his own life.

"Well, actually, all except one," Nancy said. Lexi turned to look at her, hope starting to creep back in. "He's staying and everyone else is leaving. Cars should be here for them in a couple of hours. He also asked if he could have the meeting room to stream an acoustic set for his fans."

"Yeah, we should be able to make that happen," Lexi said, turning her face from Nancy. Nancy didn't need to see the smile spreading across her face right now. What the hell was even happening? She felt like a giddy schoolgirl. She hadn't even been giddy when she was a schoolgirl.

She went back into her office and called up to his room.

"Hello." Just the sound of his saying hello made her weak in the knees.

"Hi. It's me... umm it's Lexi,"

"Mmmm, hello Lexi," he purred into the phone. He had absolutely no business sounding as sexy as he did. If his voice did that to her, there was no way she would be able to withstand the full-on assault of his sexiness tonight.

"I'm not sure what to say. Nancy told me your whole team is checking out today. I hope I didn't cause you any trouble."

"You didn't cause any trouble. I'm glad you told me. I don't want people acting on my behalf when it is not truly on my behalf. Anyway, I am glad to have a couple of days of peace and quiet."

She grinned at the phone. "Oh, and you are all set for the meeting room, acoustic, right? I don't want to disturb the other guests too much if we can help it."

"Yes, of course, it will just be a small set list of acoustics. We should be done by eight. Then we are going for dinner, right?"

"Yeah, I mean, that sounds great."

"Good, now, don't feel bad about this for a second. Do you hear me?"

"Okay," she said tentatively.

"Okay!" he said firmly. "I need to make sure we are ready to go for the streaming event tonight, but I am counting on you for dinner."

"Okay, I'll talk to you later."

She wasn't sure what had happened exactly, but it would seem she was getting rid of Jacinda. Yay. And getting to see Liam again. Also, yay. What kind of magic made all this happen? The lost driver, broken down bus, damaged venue, and now this. Magic wasn't something that Lexi believed in, but she wasn't sure how else all of this lined up to make any of this possible.

After the meeting room had been set up, Lexi stayed in her office, waiting for Jacinda to leave. They hadn't liked each other before, and they sure as hell weren't going to like each other much now. No skin off Lexi's back. She had never been one to care about what other people thought. Having a thick skin came with the territory.

But then she saw three black cars pull up from the window in her office. The group quickly loaded their suit-cases and left.

After the cars pulled out of the drive, she turned to see Liam leaning against the front desk turning in all the room keys. He winked at her and gave her a smoldering smile. She was going to melt right there on the spot.

"Hey," he glanced down at Nancy's name tag, "Nancy, do you think I might be able to have that same sandwich and salad from the place we had yesterday?"

"I think that can be arranged," she said breathlessly as her cheeks turned a dark shade of pink. Being a natural redhead, she was prone to blushing anyway, but Lexi didn't recall ever seeing her quite that shade of red. He did seem to have that effect on everyone. As he turned and left, Lexi couldn't help but chuckle as Nancy gasped and put her hand on her chest. "That man, he can make you weak in the knees just by looking at you."

"I can text Poppy the order. Do you know what he had yesterday?"

"Oh goodness me, I maybe should've asked him. I was just so flustered. I'm sorry. Should I call him?"

"No, I'll look at the menu from yesterday. We should be able to figure it out."

Lexi: Hey, what gluten-free sandwich did you make yesterday? I'm just trying to figure out what Liam ordered. He wants it again.

Poppy- Shut up, he does not!

Lexi- Yes, he does. I need to get out of here, so I will come over and get it and get myself something.

Poppy- Okay, see you in a bit. There was only one gluten-free wrap yesterday, I will make that. What do you want?

Lexi- I want a turkey pesto panini. I miss those so much after Josh left.

Poppy- We'll get those ready for you.

Lexi got her purse out from under her desk and started to dig through it to unearth her keys. "Nancy, I'm going to lunch. I'm going to go pick up Liam's lunch and grab myself a sandwich. Do you want anything?" She asked, still digging.

"Nope, I'm good," she called from the other room.

Her fingers finally made contact with the keys at the bottom of her purse. She pulled them out and tossed her phone in her bag. "Okay, Nancy, I'll be back soon."

"Take your time," she said with a smile.

As she walked out the front door, she saw Liam sitting on the porch swing. No guitar this time, just swinging and enjoying the weather. He had on his ripped jeans and chucks like he had yesterday, but now he wore a lime green shirt with a smiley face that looked a bit small. His biceps strained against it and his tattoos peaked out, and his hair was flawlessly toussled. He almost took her breath away. But when he smiled right at her, it did take her breath away.

"Where are you sneaking off to?" he asked.

"No sneaking. I am just headed out to pick up lunch," she said.

"No delivery? I didn't want you to have to go to any trouble," he said.

"Oh, it's no trouble, I got myself something too. I'll be back in a bit."

"Let me come with you." He stood and started walking towards her.

"I'm sorry?"

"Can I come with you?" He asked with a small smile. Something about this one was different from all the smiles, it looked almost bashful.

"You want to come with me?" she asked once more.

"Don't make me ask again, I'll sound desperate. Please don't make me sound desperate."

"I thought you had to get everything ready for tonight," she said.

"Done. Meeting room is set up. Everyone else is on their way back to the city. I'm done for now."

"I mean, if you want to, I guess that would be alright." Her mind was struggling for bandwidth right now. Most of it was screaming with the want, bordering on need, to be close to him. But then there was her fifteen-year-old car that needed work and was messy, taking him to her brother and Poppy. She was struggling to compute everything going on in her brain all at once.

"Are you sure?" Amusement danced across his face.

"Yeah...My car is my brother sandwich," she stuttered. As that nonsense stuttered out of her mouth, he laughed at her.

"You got some interesting song titles of your own. My car is my brother sandwich. Sounds like a hit."

"Oh my god," she said, still holding her head in her hands. Looking up, she realized he was right there. She could smell him, it was bright and citrusy but also warm, almost cinnamony. Whatever it was, she just wanted to wrap up in him and feel his warmth. That was not helping her brain to come back online. "No, I'm sorry, my brain went offline there for a minute. Probably at the thought of you in my car. But yes, we can take the car to my brother's cafe for the sandwich. If you still want to go with me."

"Well, that does make more sense. I would love to go with you if you're comfortable with that." He looked right into her eyes, the weight of his gaze settling in her. The thought of him in her personal space and life did make her nervous, but she did want to spend more time with him.

"No, it's fine. I just wanted you to know you'll meet my brother and his wife. It is going to make her day meeting you."

"Alright, then let's get going."

They made their way to the parking lot to her beat-up Kia. "Well, this is me," she said, unlocking the doors with a click. She got in and waited for him to do the same. If he had any opinions about her car, he kept them to himself, which she was happy about. She needed to text Josh that they were coming to prepare Poppy.

> Lexi - I am on my way to get lunch. Liam is coming with me just so you know.

Slipping her phone back into her purse, she put the key in the ignition and turned it on. The sight of Liam James in her car and being this close to him made the absolute absurdity of these past two days fall away. When they were like this, he was just a man. He was still the most handsome man she had ever seen, but the more she looked at him, there was another quality about him. He was beautiful. Not that he looked androgynous by any means, but he didn't seem bothered by gender expectations. It was the juxtaposition of his black tattoos against the lime green fingernail polish. He was a walking contradiction and an utter delight.

"You ready?" he asked with a patient tone.

"Yep, let's get out of here." Putting her car in reverse, she backed out and made her way out of the parking lot.

The ride through town was quiet. Liam just looked out the window, taking in the sights. As they were leaving town to go to the orchard, which was about fifteen minutes outside of town, Liam turned to her. "Not taking me out into the woods to murder me, are you? I know Jacinda's a bit much, but this seems excessive."

"It will be a slow torturous death... death by gluten," she said with a straight face.

"No! I can feel my stomach cramping already!" he said laughing at her. She chuckled at him. There was an ease to their banter, which was new. It was nice to be able to complete a thought around him and not be a tongue-tied mess.

"But seriously, where are we going? I assumed the cafe was in town."

"Oh, no. My sister-in-law's family runs an apple orchard

a bit out of town. She and my brother run the cafe. It shouldn't be too busy, early summer isn't a normally busy time for the orchard."

"I gotcha. Sounds fun."

They pulled up to the orchard and Lexi stopped and took a breath. She was nervous. Why was she nervous? She was getting way ahead of herself with this whole Liam thing.

"Okay, so just FYI my sister-in-law is delightful. But she is a fan and has a pretty big personality, so I'm just warning you now."

"Oh, that's nice. I look forward to meeting her."

"She is clearly looking forward to meeting you too." She pointed to Poppy who was standing in the front of the store nearly vibrating off the ground. "Let's get this over with," said Lexi, dread sounding in her voice.

They got out of the car and headed to the cafe.

"Hi, Poppy. This is Liam, but you clearly know that."

Liam reached out and took her hand and smiled his stupid smile that could light up an entire arena. Poppy opened her mouth to speak but all that came out was a little squeal.

Josh came around the corner from the cafe. "Hey, are you guys eating here or should I bag up your sandwiches?"

Lexi looked at Liam.

"We can eat here if you have time, that is. I don't want to keep you from your work," he said.

Something about his thoughtfulness settled inside of her. He was a constant surprise. "Okay, I guess we'll eat here," said Lexi.

Looking over at Poppy, who was still standing there vibrating and smiling, Josh laughed. "Has she been like this since you guys got here?"

"Yep..." Lexi said.

"Don't worry, it doesn't last long. So, this is the handsome man from the photograph?" Liam asked.

"Yeah, this is my brother Josh... Josh, this is Liam."

Josh stuck out his hand and gave him a firm handshake. "Nice to me you," he said with his quintessential Josh smile.

"You too. I've really been enjoying getting to know your sister."

Josh's eyes narrow for the slightest second. "She's the best. I'm just glad you got her out of that office. I haven't seen her in weeks," he said very pointedly at her.

"I know, I've been busy, and you and Poppy are working on the house. But I'll be there this weekend."

"You better be. Let me finish up your food. Sit anywhere you like."

They all walked into the cafe, passing through the store. "Your family owns this orchard?" Liam asked Poppy, clearly trying to include her.

She had followed them in but still hadn't said anything. Lexi was amused by this. She hadn't seen Poppy speechless or shy since... well ever if she really thought about it.

"Yeah... I make the muffins," she stuttered out.

"Oh, those were good. Being gluten-free I've had some terrible muffins, but those were the best."

"Poppy does make the best muffins," Josh said, giving Poppy a sly smile. He set down the two plates he was carrying in front of them.

"What can I get you to drink?" asked Josh.

"Waters is good for me," Liam said. Poppy had just started to recover, but it seemed she was stuck again, smiling stupidly at him.

"I'll get you guys some water," Josh said with a smile as

he went back into the kitchen, dragging Poppy along with him.

"So, that's your brother?" he asked.

"That's my brother."

"Is this the first time you've been here?"

"Technically yes, but to be fair they did just open," she said trying to justify it. If she was opening a new business, Josh would have been there on opening day, and would have been her biggest cheerleader. Guilt started to eat at her. Maybe she should spend a little more time with him, she just didn't want to intrude on their time as a new couple.

Poppy and Josh came out of the kitchen and Poppy seemed to be her normal self.

"I heard your bus broke down. How long are you stuck in town for?" Poppy asked.

"I think the bus will be fixed by tomorrow, but I am planning on staying here until Sunday. I have a concert in the city on Monday, so I'll head in for that, but I wanted to stay here. I'm looking for a town to film my video for Home and I think Mystic Falls might be a perfect fit."

"Really? That would be incredible. It's a great little town," said Poppy.

"So it would seem, and I would love to get to those waterfalls I can see from my window at the inn. I think that's the next item on my agenda."

"I'm sorry you didn't make it to the falls this morning. You really should've just kept going," Lexi said. She was feeling a little guilty that she had kept him from exploring. These past two days had flipped her world on its head, and right now she was just struggling to keep up. It just felt like ever since he had waltzed into Mystic Falls, she hadn't been able to find her footing.

"Don't you dare apologize. I needed to know what Jacinda was up to. Plus, you would have signed that ridiculous NDA."

Lexi looked down at her lap. In what world does a pop star come to Mystic Falls and then almost kiss her on a porch swing and then tell his manager to leave for treating her badly?

"What NDA?" Josh asked in a tone that sounded like a big brother, even though he was a little brother. For them things were even a bit more complicated because Lexi had basically raised Josh since they were teenagers.

"It's nothing," she said, unsure of what to say.

"People don't have to sign NDAs for nothing Lexi. What's going on?" He eyed Liam suspiciously.

"Josh, really it's nothing." She didn't know what else to say. She wouldn't tell Josh about the moment on the porch swing because that seemed like it would be a violation of Liam's privacy. The very thing she was going to have to sign the NDA about.

"My manager, who may no longer be my manager, was apparently making anyone I talked to sign an NDA. I'll get to the bottom of it, but for now, I sent everyone back to the city, so it is just me here for a couple of days. I'm really looking forward to enjoying Mystic Falls. What are some things you think I should check out before I leave?" He asked.

Lexi smiled at his very diplomatic subject change. He was so goddamn charming it was almost unnerving.

"Well, you should definitely see the town square. The gazebo and the shops really give it a nice feel," Josh said, finally relaxing.

Liam smiled at him, "Thanks, I'll definitely check that out."

"Oh, and if you really want to get the feel of small-town life you should come to our cookout this weekend. My brother and his husband and my best friend and her husband will be there. It will be great!" Poppy blurted out.

"Poppy, I think Liam has better things to do than come to our cookout," Josh said as he lovingly rubbed his wife's hand.

"No, actually that would be really great. I'd love to go. That is if you don't mind, of course," he said to Lexi.

"Yeah, I mean if you want to, you can for sure go."

"You will be there, right?" he asked her.

"She will be there. She promised," Josh said firmly.

"Great! Count us in!" said Liam.

They finished up lunch and chatted. Things felt surprisingly normal and pleasant. Lexi almost forgot Liam was a superstar.

"Well, I better get back to work. And I'm sure Liam has many other things he should be doing," she said.

They made their way back to the car. Lexi stopped to watch him as he got in. Something about this felt normal. She wasn't sure why or even how, but it did. Looking at him, she saw the person she had seen on magazine covers and on her tv, but she also saw him for what he was. He was just a man. A man she had googled many times, but never opened any of the articles because it felt like a violation of his privacy. She wanted to know more about him. And she really wanted to kiss him. And she somehow got the idea he wanted that too, which was a surreal feeling. He was a superstar who could have literally anyone he wanted, but he seemed to want her, which was so hard for her to fathom. Not because she didn't think she deserved love, because she did, but it was just... him.

He opened the door of her car and turned to catch her

looking at him. He stopped and smiled at her. "Whatcha thinkin'?" He asked.

"I was just thinking about how surreal this whole thing is. Two days ago, if you would have told me all this would happen, I would have thought you were insane."

As Lexi was pulling on her seat belt Liam looked at her, with an unreadable expression on his face. "I'm not one to believe everything happens for a reason. But there does seem to be something deeper going on. My bus breaks down in this small town, hundreds of miles off course, my bus driver still can't figure out what happened there. The arena for tonight's show took damage from the storm and so I ended up having a few days off, which I haven't had in months. There just seem to be a lot of coincidences."

"I know I have to get back to work, but why don't I take the long way back? I can show you some of the great spots around town. So clearly, this is the orchard. This is one of the major spots of town, especially in the past few years. I'm just going to text Nancy and let her know I'll be a little late."

Opening her purse, Lexi started to dig her phone out to send the text. Liam's hands covered her's and her heart skipped a beat. She looked up at him, his face was mere inches from his and she instinctually licked her lips. His eyes fell to her lips, and she thought for a moment he was going to kiss her. She wanted him to kiss her. His thumb gently rubbed over her hand.

"I don't want to keep you from work, but I would love to explore the town with you."

"Okay," she said. Her phone, which was still buried in her purse, vibrated. It snapped her out of this moment, whatever was happening here needed to be figured out. She needed a minute to breathe. She continued to dig for her phone, and he moved his hand.

Poppy- Is there something going on
between you and LIAM JAMES???!!!

Lexi just couldn't with this right now. She shot a text to Nancy letting her know she would be back a little later than anticipated and started up the car.

"Well, let the tour commence," she said.

They drove off and Lexi took them through town. She showed him the picturesque landscape of the town square. Main street that had all the little shops, bookstore, Fipp's Market, and town meeting hall where the drama and fun of this small town took place. As they turned off the square Twistee's came into view They had the best chili dogs and ice cream in town.

"Is that building a giant ice cream cone?" Liam asked.

"It is. Do you want some ice cream?"

"Yeah, I do!"

"Well then let's go." Lexi turned into the parking lot.

"This town has such great vibes," Liam said, taking it all in.

"It really does. It's been a great place to live." And she meant that. Lexi wasn't one of those people who was always looking for their way out of their hometown. This town had saved her life quite literally. Things hadn't always been easy for her and Josh, and this town had helped them.

"What do you want?" he asked.

"I'll get our ice cream," Lexi said, pulling out her wallet. He looked at her with a look that said, 'Put that away right now. I am a superstar, and I will buy your ice cream.' She looked down. Something about this squeezed at her heart. This seemingly small gesture of the complete normalcy of getting ice cream together gave her an unfamiliar cozy feeling.

"A twist cone, please," she said with a small smile.

Liam went up to the window and ordered a twist cone and a cup of chocolate ice cream.

"Shall we?" he asked, motioning his head toward the picnic tables.

She followed and sat next to him. She took a lick of her cone and looked over to see him with a slight hunger in his gaze. That couldn't be right. He held her gaze as he slowly took a bite of his ice cream, flipping the spoon in his mouth and slowly dragging it between his lips. The mere act of eating ice cream had never done this to her before. Squeezing her thighs and squirming in her seat she looked away from him. He chuckled.

Reaching into his pocket he pulled out his phone, he held it out like he wanted to take a picture with her.

"I won't have to sign an NDA, will I?" she joked.

"Get over here," he said playfully.

She scooted over and he snapped their picture. His body pressed against hers. After he was done with the picture he didn't move away. They sat there, thighs touching, finishing their ice cream.

"Is this even real?" she said.

"What do you mean?" He asked.

"You? This? Whatever is happening?"

He pulled back and looked directly into her eyes, it pulled her up short and took her breath away. Just a look from him stopped her heart and the smile started it thudding in her chest again.

"It certainly feels real to me," he said. He looked away and cleared his throat.

They both finished their ice cream in relative silence, sitting next to each other, legs still pressed firmly together.

Chapter 9

Liam

Liam just finished up the set he was streaming for his fans. He had gotten on and apologized for the cancellation and sincerely hoped everyone would be able to make the rescheduled concert. Then he played a set of six songs that lent themselves well to acoustic covers. He took his time to connect with his fans. He didn't often get to speak with them and perform for them on such an intimate stage, so that was nice. Performing on a big stage had its perks, but sometimes little moments where he could play in a more intimate setting felt good. But he was a little distracted, his mind drifting to what was after this, taking Lexi out to dinner.

He was drawn to her in a way he hadn't been drawn to anybody in a very long time. It was hard to connect with people on a personal level. Connection was something that used to come easy to him, but it just didn't anymore. After everything with Henry and the way his team tried to do damage control on the situation, he wasn't surprised he'd lost his touch. But maybe part of the reason he hadn't been able to connect to people now was because team of people around him kept him separate from people.

Were they controlling who got close to him? After that scandal when Henry had left, Liam was lost. The label talked him into getting rid of Sue, who had been his manager since he first got out to LA. Ever since he lost Henry and Sue, it almost felt like he was two people. Like he was losing the real him in the creation of Liam James. It was hard enough to make real connections in this industry, even without people getting in his way. He needed to get to the bottom of this, but first, he was going to take Lexi out to dinner. Even with all this going on, whenever he tried to focus, his thoughts always seemed to return to those piercing blue eyes and full round ass.

He had wanted to order a car and take her out like he would if he was taking her out in the city, but she refused. She would be driving them to a little bistro for dinner. It wasn't quite how he had grown accustomed to wining and dining people, but if he was honest, she wasn't the type of people he usually wined and dined.

It had nothing to do with who she was or what she looked like, but he normally didn't find himself in these types of circles. These small towns are a close-knit circle of people. He had grown up with this but hadn't had it for himself in years. It felt comforting after being in the artificial show business for the past five years. He didn't take his success for granted and enjoyed many of the privileges that came with his new life, but he missed this sometimes.

He finished up, closed his laptop, and turned off all the ring lights. Once everything was cleaned up, he went to his room to drop some things off. When he came down, Lexi was in the reception area. He watched as she talked to the second-shift front desk clerk. The clerk was showing her a picture of her baby and Lexi was cooing at the cuteness. The genuine nature of the interaction pulled at his heart. Genuine connection had been sorely missing in his life and Lexi was one of the most genuine people he had ever known. He didn't even really know her, but he could tell by how she talked to him and everyone else around her. There was something about her he couldn't get enough of.

Also, he couldn't help but notice her ass as she leaned over the desk to give the clerk back her phone. She was wearing a tighter skirt than he had seen on her previously, and he really wanted to lift it up and take her from behind. He closed his eyes and shook that thought from his head. His sexual attraction had always been based on the person, and he was attracted to Lexi on a level he had never experienced before. He was pretty sure she felt it too, and if she was willing, he hoped she might want to come back to his room tonight. Of course, that would be up to her. If she wanted that, he needed to be honest with her at dinner and make sure she knew what she was getting into. But he wanted to ruck up that skirt and taste her more than anything. Just the thought had him adjusting his pants.

He leaned against the doorway and watched their interaction for a bit longer. The desk clerk looked up at him and jumped a little, and Lexi turned. When she saw him, she smiled and tucked her hair behind her ears as a flush crept up her chest. Which then drew his attention from her glorious round ass to the deep cleavage of her shirt. Dinner and talking, and then maybe all the dirty thoughts running through his mind could be acted on.

"Hi," she said breathlessly. "Are you ready to go?"

"Lead the way," he said, gesturing to the door. Pulling it open, he held the door open as she stepped through. There was a bit of chill in the air for a night in mid-June, but with his ongoing thoughts about this woman before him, the chill was a welcome distraction. He was kicking himself for not calling a car service, imagining the fun they could have in the back of a car, but instead, he followed her to her car and got in.

She drove them to the center of town. The town square and gazebo were lit up with fairy lights. The little Italian bistro was only a block off the main square. Inside, there was violin music and red checkered tablecloths. It was dimly lit with a candle on every table.

"I checked. They do have a few gluten-free options," she said as she wrung her hands. She looked nervous, and that just wouldn't do. He wanted her to be comfortable around him. So, few people were, and he really hoped she might be one of them.

"This place is great," he said. He took her by the hand as the hostess led them to a small table in the back. Once they were at their table, he pulled out her chair and scooted it in as she sat down. She looked up and smiled at him, and he fought every urge to kiss her perfect mouth right then. There would be time for that he reminded himself.

"So, what do you think of Mystic Falls so far?" asked Lexi nervously as she took a piece of bread from the breadbasket the waitress had brought after they placed their orders.

"I think it's incredible. I believe it'll be a great place to film my video for Home. Are you familiar with that song?" he asked.

Lexi looked down at the bread in her hands and then back up at him with a sheepish smile. Shaking her head, "No, I'm not. I'm afraid I don't know much of your music. I hope that is okay?"

"Well, honestly, I figured that out when you didn't

recognize any of my song titles last night." He would be lying to himself if he said he didn't have jitters, but they were normal jitters. In fact, he was most surprised about how normal things felt. Being around someone who didn't know anything about him was refreshing.

"Yeah, I went home and googled you," she said with a smile.

His heart dropped. She had googled him. What had she found out? While he wasn't ashamed of anything he had done or any of the people he had been with, the media has a way of twisting things. Making it seem like he was a villain when he wasn't. Making it seem like something was immoral when it was a perfectly normal part of the sexual human experience. He would rather have had that talk, be upfront rather than trying to explain and fight the negative twists the media put on his past.

"I saw some salacious headlines, and I know gossip sites are awful, so I just stopped. It seems almost like an invasion of privacy to delve that deeply into someone's past when they are already bearing their souls in their art. I think people should be able to choose the parts of themselves that they share and those they keep private. We all have pasts we want to keep private." She took a sip of wine.

Liam couldn't believe it. Was this girl for real?

"You saw some of those headlines and didn't read the articles?" he asked.

"Well, to be fair, I only opened one about your dating past. But the headline questioned your sexuality, and I thought this is not my business. So, no, I didn't continue to read."

"What if I wanted it to be your business?" He asked in a low, raspy voice.

"What?" She squeaked and squirmed.

"There is clearly some sexual tension here," he said as he reached his hand across the table to hers, tracing his fingers along the back of her knuckles.

"You can't be serious," she said with a surprising matter-of-factness to her voice. Lexi's eyes darted around the room, but Liam was already aware they were alone in a deserted, dimly lit dining room.

"Oh, I most certainly am. Are you going to tell me I am the only one who feels it?" He watched her squirm with a cocked eyebrow, knowing exactly what he was doing to her.

"Of course, I feel it. But you're this superstar sex symbol, and I'm just an average, fat inn manager from small town USA."

"You're beautiful."

"I didn't say I wasn't beautiful. I said I was fat," she said with her chin set for defiance.

"Yes, you are. And I want to learn your body, explore every curve and know what makes you moan."

Her mouth fell open, and she just sat there gaping at him.

Soon the waitress came and brought their dinner. His chicken and roasted Italian veggies and her plate of carbonara. He told the waitress how good everything looked and thanked her, all while Lexi still sat there staring at him, her cheeks red. In his mind, he swept all the food off this table and pulled her on top of it and feasted on her instead.

He picked up her hand and pressed an innocent kiss to her knuckles, enjoying how thoroughly undone she was already.

"Let's eat, then you can come back to my room."

Her eyes flickered, and she seemed to come crashing back to reality. "I can't do that!" she protested.

"And why not, if we both want it," he said, trying not to sound as desperate as he was.

"I work there. I'm the boss. I can't have a hook-up at the inn," she said. Liam was trying to figure this out. Car sex was off the table because he wanted to worship her body. That would not do what he had in mind any justice. He was tempted to close down this restaurant and pay them just to let him have his way with her right here, but that still wasn't right. Even he had to admit there would need to be NDAs for that. But his want was bordering on need for this woman.

"Well, I know it's not as nice as the places you usually stay, but you could come back to my place," she said tentatively.

"Perfect. Now, let's eat. I have plans for us later."

The flush crept over her cheeks once again. His erection was straining painfully in his pants. He had to stop and close his eyes and picture something else... puppies, cute St. Bernard puppies, playing in a suitcase. The only surefire way to make his erection go away because if he kept down his current path, he would come in his pants before dinner was over. For now, he would be a gentleman, show her a wonderful time, and engage in thoughtful discussion. Lexi was as fascinating as she was attractive, and he wanted to know more about her. He could save his current train of thought for later tonight.

Chapter 10

Lexi

Liam held out his hand and helped Lexi from her chair. He was not at all what she initially thought. He had come on strong. So strong she was almost lightheaded from the blood all suddenly leaving her head and rushing places it had no business going, but then he seemed to change. She was hoping he hadn't changed his mind because she really wanted to do the things he was talking about. But she wouldn't be surprised if he changed his mind because look at him.

This wasn't a 'poor me, who would ever want me?' type of thought. This was a very realistic thought. They were from two completely separate worlds and on two completely separate levels. This was a fancy date to her, but she was more of a 'pajamas and movies' kind of a girl. She would make them cute pj's, sexy pj's even, but she didn't feel like she was on his level. He was on the 'supermodels and private jets to Paris' level. She had never even left New York. The fanciest thing she had ever done was stay a night in the city to see a Broadway show. What would they even have in common? Of course, he had changed his mind.

Although, he did hold her hand as they walked to her car, and the feeling that danced between their clasped hands was magic.

Once they were in her car, she took a breath trying to collect her thoughts.

"Where to?" she asked as nonchalantly as possible, even though inside she was screaming *please say you still want to come home with me.*

Confusion danced behind his eyes as he looked at her. "I thought we had this all figured out, gorgeous. You're taking me home. Unless you have changed your mind, which is totally your prerogative. No Pressure."

"No! I still want to. I just wasn't sure if you wanted to."

"Oh... I still want to," he said as he brushed a lock of hair behind her ear. The zing that went through her body every time they touched was like nothing she had ever experienced before. Their eyes locked. As she looked into his deep brown eyes, the world fell away, the only thing that existed was them, and the electric connection pulling them together.

"I have to kiss you." His hand slid under her jaw and into her hair. The air felt heavy with anticipation and desire. Her heart was pounding in her chest, and she felt a bit lightheaded. "Can I kiss you?" he asked, then ran his tongue across his bottom lip.

She nodded, unable to speak.

He closed the distance between them. His face was now mere inches from hers, much like it had been last night on the porch swing, but this time she knew what was coming. This time she could see his face. Her heart was pounding out of her chest. *Don't wake up.* She thought to herself, afraid this was a dream.

He stilled and looked at her. No. No no no. This was a

dream.

"What was that?" he asked, his smile creasing the lines next to his eyes that were still so close to hers.

"What?" She asked, unable to complete a thought.

"You just said something."

"No, I didn't"

He gently laughed, "Yes, you did."

Oh, fuck. Did she say that out loud? There was nothing left to do. She closed the distance between them, her lips crashing into his. His hand that had been cradling her head fisted and tugged at her hair. He opened his mouth, deepening the kiss between them. She let him take control. His tongue entered her mouth with delicious deliberation, and she couldn't hold back her moan. He started to pull away, but she chased his mouth, not ready for this to end.

He remained close, pulling his mouth away and leaning his forehead against hers. "Please tell me you live close by."

"I'm five minutes away."

"Too far," he said, his breath against her cheek. "Get there faster."

Pulling her head away, she put the car into reverse and tried not to squeal out of there. Liam's possessive hand rested firmly on her thigh, as if to remind her of his intentions, if she were to forget them again.

They pulled up to her house. It was a little run-down, two-story house. It was the house she had grown up in. She and Josh had lived here together their entire lives until Josh moved out a few months ago. She was happy for Josh, but she did miss him. Maybe that was why she had been pulling away. But that was a thought for later. Right now, her thoughts were a little preoccupied with the hand on her thigh that was slowly venturing higher.

"Well, this is it. I'm sure you are used to much nicer

accommodations," she said, the nerves sinking back in as hard as she tried to fight them.

"Lexi, I wasn't always who I am now. I've only been this guy for the past five years. I spent much more time as a guy growing up in a house not much bigger than this one with my sister. We have much more in common than you seem to think." He reached for her face again and cupped her jaw as he put another sizzling kiss on her lips. "Now can we please go inside? I can't wait another minute to have you alone."

She opened her door while his lips were still on her. Soon, his kiss trailed down her jaw and neck until he was kissing that spot where her neck met her shoulder, driving her over the edge. "Let's go in."

They both got out of the car and made their way up the stairs to the front door. Lexi was trying to unlock the door as Liam's hand rested on the small of her back. She was still pinching herself. Liam James was about to come into her house. LIAM JAMES was about to come into her house. The house that was in desperate need of sprucing. It felt a lot like she did, stuck in time.

"Are you okay?" he whispered in her ear, sensing her apprehension.

"Yep. I'm fine. Let's do this." She unlocked the door and they walked in. Her nerves bubbled under the surface until Liam spun her and slammed the door behind them as he pulled her close. His mouth connected with her, and she instantly forgot to be nervous. The only emotion there was any room for in this moment was lust, pure lust.

His mouth ravaged her, and he sucked on her tongue. His hand slowly let go of her waist and began to explore the rest of her body. They roamed her back, still holding her close. She bit his bottom lip and he moaned. She had elicited a moan from Liam James. The thought of that did things to her. The feel of his erection pressing into her belly did things to her too. Panty ruining things. She hadn't had sex in a long time... too long to figure out at this moment, but this was one hell of a way to break a dry spell.

She pulled back in an attempt to catch her breath, and to look at him. He was so very nice to look at.

"I'm going to need you naked and on a bed. Right now."

"Follow me," she said in the sultriest tone she could muster and led him to her bedroom.

Walking away from him and leading him into her room gave her time to stop and think about one very important element that was missing from tonight. They got into her room, and she opened her bedside drawer hoping for a miracle. Crap.

"Ummm Liam, you wouldn't happen to have a condom?"

His face fell, "No. I do back at the inn, but not on me."

"Well shit, should we go get one?"

"No," he said, his mouth finding her neck again.

"No?"

"If you're willing, there are many other things we can do to bring each other pleasure. We'll have a condom next time."

"Next time?"

"Next time. I'm here for a couple more days and I plan for a lot more next times before I leave." At that he pulled away and took his shirt off. She had seen him with his shirt off on plenty of pictures from her limited google search, but it was nothing compared to a shirtless Liam James here in her room. She couldn't look away. Reaching out she traced one of his many tattoos, this one was a black swallow that sat right above his pec.

He put his hand over hers and held it there. She could

feel his heart pounding beneath. It matched the rhythm of her own heart pounding away in her chest. With his other hand he cupped her face, and this time pressed a gentle barely there kiss to her mouth. This tenderness was not what she was expecting from their encounter, but she liked it all the same.

His hand drifted down until he gently tugged at the hem of her shirt. "May I?" he asked. She nodded and he lifted the hem and dragged it up and over her head. By the time she was free of her shirt she saw his eyes glazed over with lust staring at her chest. She reached behind her back and undid the clasp of her bra and slowly let the straps fall over her shoulders before discarding the garment entirely.

"You are so beautiful." His hand came up and held her breast, gently pinching the nipple between his fingers. She turned and Liam's fingers found the zipper on the back of her skirt. He pulled it down. Lexi faced him and shimmied the skirt over her hips. He stepped back and looked at her, his hands undoing the belt of his pants. Something about the way he looked at her made her want to cover up. Looking at him, at his perfection, only made her more aware of the belly roll her underwear was covering, and the stretch marks that lined her belly, thighs and breasts. She wanted to dive under the covers or turn out the lights but settled for moving her arms across herself.

"Don't you dare," he said, pulling her arms wide and taking her in. "You're perfect and I can't wait to taste you." Stepping out of his pants he sat down on the bed and positioned her between his legs. His erection straining against his boxer briefs was enough to help her regain her confidence. Then his mouth found her nipple, and everything fell away. All she felt was his hands exploring her body and his mouth fully drawing her nipple into his mouth.

She laughed.

"What on earth are you laughing at?" he asked, then lightly bit her nipple.

"Just that this is real. This. This is happening. I never could have dreamed of it. And if I could have, it wouldn't have held a candle to you, the actual you, in my bed."

"Get in this bed with me," he said as he yanked her down, pulling her on top of him. And at that, all the humor and everything else left her head. Burned away by the feel of his erection between her legs only separated by two thin pieces of fabric. He rolled her onto her back and knelt between her legs. His hands traced her plush thighs. She reached her own hands up, running them over his chest and arms and all the tattoos that covered them. Bending back down he caged her with his arms on either side and kissed her. Hard. This kiss was filled with passion. More passion than any of the previous kisses. She ran her hands up and down his back, feeling his muscles shift as his body moved.

He moved his hand down over her breast and plucked the nipple to a peak, licking it as he did. His hand kept moving south over the mound of her belly until he was cupping her sex. He ground his palm into her clit. Even with his hand on the outside of her underwear, she worried she might just come right there on the spot.

He grabbed the elastic of her underwear and pulled. She shifted her hips so he could guide them down. Then he sat up between her legs and pushed them wide. Lexi watched as he looked at her, licking his lips. She gasped as he traced a finger down her seam. He looked up at her, making eye contact as he pushed his fingers into her folds, dipping in and out until he moved to her clit and rubbed a small circle. She moaned, already feeling an orgasm building inside.

One finger slid inside while his other hand was still slowly working her clit. Holy fuck. Then he slid in two, then three. He found this spot inside and her whole body convulsed. The press there started to increase, and she couldn't stop herself. She started moving against his hand, grinding on them. Then she felt it, the orgasm that had been building inside of her came tearing through her. She cried out and he was there. Working her through every wave, bringing her more pleasure than she had ever felt.

When she finally came down, he looked at her and licked his fingers. "Has anyone ever told you how pretty you are when you come?"

Lexi shook her head. There were still no words to be found.

"Well, that's a damn shame. Ya know what else is a damn shame, I won't be able to see you come this time." At that he lowered his mouth and kissed her seam. He pressed a gentle kiss before holding her open with his hands and licking her slowly from her entrance all the way up to that little bundle of nerves. The feeling set her on fire. The magnetism between them was powerful, but this was pure lust. This was someone who knew what he was doing, and Lexi was going to come again soon. She could already feel it building deep inside of her.

He licked her slowly once more. Then he slid two fingers inside of her working her like he had, finding the precise spot that had made her moan previously. His tongue began working small circles around her clit and she began to rock against his mouth. She couldn't seem to help herself. He growled and pulled his fingers out of her and then wrapped his arms around her thighs and roughly pulled her down the bed, just a little bit, enough to surprise her. He didn't let go, holding her firm and still, his fingers digging in the softness of her inner thighs. He was in total control and Lexi was just about to lose herself again. She reached down and fisted her hand in his hair holding him close to her. He sucked her clit into his mouth and that was enough to send her hurdling over the edge. She cried out and convulsed as he continued to lick her. Finally, she pushed his head away and laid panting on the bed.

"Holy crap, that was incredible," she said breathlessly.

Liam crawled up the bed until he was right next to her. He gathered her onto his chest and stroked her hair. Closing her eyes, Lexi thanked whatever force on this earth that had made this possible. This kind of thing didn't happen to her. It just didn't. Yet here she was in her own bed, with Liam James who gave her two of the best orgasms she has ever had. And what was even weirder than that was how normal it all felt. How comfortable she felt with him.

"What are you thinking?" He asked lightly, stroking her arms.

"Just how unreal this all seems," she said. No use trying to hide it or be coy. Being coy had never been her style anyway. "I woke up yesterday and went into the diner like it was any other day, and then today, here I am. This isn't the kind of thing that generally happens to me. I don't quite know how to take all of it."

"I hear ya. These types of things don't happen to me either," he said.

Turning, Lexi rested her chin on her hand that was laying across her chest. "You mean you don't hook up with small town inn managers everywhere you go?"

"No. Actually, this is a first for me," he said, amusement seeping into his voice and a slow smile creeping across his face. Not the public smile, given she loved that one too, but so did millions of other people. This smile she hadn't seen before. It felt like it was just for her. "I know I have this reputation of being a sexually fluid playboy... and while I can't really disagree, it's just not really who I am anymore."

"The sexually fluid or the playboy part?" Lexi asked, trying to make him laugh.

"Oh no, I'm still sexually fluid. I claim to be bi, or maybe pan. But really, sexuality and who I'm attracted to varies so much from person to person, it's hard to pin down. It's about the person, not the gender. That's one of the reasons I refuse to talk about it. Number one, because it is nobody's business who I sleep with, but also because I'm not really about labeling it."

He had been lazily stroking her arm this whole time. While she hadn't known that about him, it wasn't really a surprise. He kind of had that aura about him and one of the headlines she saw when she did that short google search addressed his sexuality and past sexual partners. That was the one that made her stop searching. That information shouldn't just be there for anyone to find. It was personal.

"But the playboy part is one I'm not anymore. I was, believe me. I had my fair share of partners and places. I like sex, and I enjoyed it with many people. I don't regret or feel shame for any of that. I do regret that sometimes being with me can bring people scrutiny or attention they didn't want. That's why I stopped. I live a crazy life and I just don't want to bring anyone into the tornado that is Liam James. Believe it or not, I haven't had sex in over a year."

"Really? I mean, I haven't either, but we lead very different lives," she said, sounding a little surprised.

"That we do." He kissed her temple and breathed her in.

"Can I ask you something?" She asked.

"Anything."

"Why are you telling me all this? I mean, I appreciate it.

I'm enjoying my time getting to know you. But you just told me you are a private person because of your past, yet we've known each other for two days and you just told me all of that. I could run and tell TMZ."

"But you wouldn't," he said so surely.

"You're right, I absolutely would not. But how are you so sure?"

"I just feel it. I haven't felt the level of attraction I feel for you in a very long time. And if I'm being honest, it feels different than anything I've ever felt before. I don't really know how to describe it."

"I feel it too." She laid her head against his chest and listened to his heart beating, and again she noticed their hearts kept perfect time. It was almost as if their hearts were connected. "Did you know our hearts are beating at the same time?"

"Are they?" he said as he took a deep breath.

"They are. They were last time too. That's a strange coincidence."

"I don't believe in coincidences. I can't explain any of this, but it is not a coincidence."

She didn't know what to do with any of the information she had just gotten, but she did know she was lying on the chest of a man who had just given her two mind blowing orgasms and it was time she returned the favor. She traced her fingers down his muscular chest and continued lower to the band of his boxer briefs. She lifted her head and kissed him. When she deepened the kiss, he met her, but made no attempt to take the lead. He was going to let her lead this portion of the evening and she was more than happy to do so. She started to kiss down his jaw, feeling the rough stubble on her lips. The abrasiveness felt nice in contrast to the smoothness of the rest of his skin. She continued kissing lower, sliding her hand under his boxers and wrapping her hand around his cock.

She shifted and pulled at his waist band. He helped her take them off, and there she was. Sitting next to this naked, beautiful man. It had been too long. She stroked him again and he arched into her hand. This was going to be fun. She dropped her head and swirled her tongue around the head as she continued to stroke him.

"Fuck," he groaned out. Looking up at him, she sucked a little more of him into her mouth, never breaking eye contact. His eyes burned through her. They were so full of lust. She popped off and stroked him again. The little bead of pre-cum at the head spurred her on. She bent her head down and took all of him in until he hit the back of her throat. He groaned again and his hand fisted in her hair. Pulling up she swirled her tongue around the tip one more time then got to work. She wanted him to come. She wanted him to come as hard as she had. He started rocking into her mouth. Her eyes began to water as he hit the back of her throat, but the noises he made were pure heaven.

"Lexi, I'm going to come," he rasped out. She took him in deeply and with a loud groan and his hand fisted in her hair he released down the back of her throat, and she swallowed it all down.

She looked up at him. His eyes were squeezed shut and his breathing was labored. "Good?" she asked in an innocent tone.

"So. Fucking. Good. I can't wait until tomorrow. I am going to fuck you so good."

"Is that a promise?" She asked as she moved to rest on his chest again.

Pulling her face towards, he kissed her. "It's more than a promise, it's a fucking vow."

Chapter 11

Liam

Liam stretched and looked at the clock. It was three-thirty in the morning. He had slept for three hours. He and Lexi had fallen asleep after she had given him what might have been the best blow job of his entire life. And here she was, her head on his chest and leg draped over him, making the softest cutest little snores he had ever heard. He couldn't help but smile and kiss her head. He couldn't describe what it was he felt for this woman. He had never felt anything like it before. Sure, he had been in love, but that always felt like a drug, felt like this thrill and need. Yet, here was tenderness and love. All the other times sent him into orbit, whereas this seemed to ground him.

He reached beside the bed for his jeans to get the phone out of his pocket as carefully as he could to not wake her. He had been MIA for most of the day except for the private show he had done. It went well, but it was nice to let that world fall away for a little bit. He couldn't remember the last time he felt this, for lack of a better word, normal. But he needed to check back in with the circus he usually lived in.

He unlocked his phone, and he had twenty text messages, most of them from Jacinda. Some of them apologizing, some checking on the show, others demanding he text her back. He closed out of them before replying. That was not what he was going to do right now. Instead, he checked his email. Things with the tour seemed to be getting back on track. The buses were all fixed and accounted for. All that was left to do was take a car to the city on Sunday. Tomorrow was Friday... well today was Friday he supposed, so he still had some time.

There was also an email from his sister. His family were the only other people who still made him feel like his life had any sense of normalcy. Well, until Lexi.

He ignored the rest and opened the email from his sister.

Hey Liam, I know you are busy being fancy pants McGee over there, but your nephew's birthday is in three weeks. We already have the gift you sent and once again you are always over the top. He'll love it, but I wanted to invite you to the party. I don't expect you to make it, but you're always invited. I attached the invite. We would love to facetime with you when you get a chance that weekend. Let us know what works. Love you Lots - Lauren.

He made a mental note to check his schedule and email his sister back tomorrow. He would love to be able to go to his nephew's birthday party. That was something normal uncles did. When he was with his family, he didn't have to be Liam James he could just be himself. Sometime over the years his life had started to feel split into two separate people, Liam James and Liam Sheffield, and lately Liam James was taking over everything.

He loved his life. He couldn't live without music and song writing, but he also felt dedicated to his fans. His shows were a place for safe self-expression, anyone could be whoever they wanted to be at a Liam James concert. It was the team around him personally that had gotten a bit dicey lately.

He had never felt any shame about his life until the label started treating him like there was something to be ashamed of. They wanted him to appeal to a wider audience, but he wasn't sure he wanted to appeal to a larger audience. He hadn't quite figured out how to be for everyone but still be himself.

He wondered if Lexi would like to come meet his family... Woah. He wasn't sure where that thought had come from. This thing with her, as awesome as it was, couldn't last. He couldn't pull her into the Liam James life. Lexi was amazing but he could tell she'd a troubled past. While she hadn't shared much of her past with him, it was a gift he had, sensing people's pain. That is part of what helped him write his music, but it also made things difficult for him. He had been sensitive like that his entire life.

He should leave. He should get back to the city, but he couldn't bring himself to leave her. The draw he felt was inexplicable, but that was all the more reason he needed to leave. He wouldn't bring scandal to another person. And as beautiful as he found her, he dealt with the media all the time. They wouldn't be kind to her, and he refused to put her through that. Still, he couldn't bring himself to leave. But right now, he didn't need to. Right now, he had a sleeping woman on his chest and that kind of trumped all things he should be doing.

So, he took his phone and snapped a picture of this moment. Of him in her bed and her sleeping on his bare chest, arms wrapped around him. This moment may not last, they both had real worlds they needed to go back to, but he would always have this memory. And he had vowed to fuck her tomorrow and that wasn't something he planned to back out of. Was it a good idea? Probably not. But he didn't care. He was only here for a few more days and he would be upfront with her about everything, but if she was willing to be with him for those three days knowing that's all it was and all it could be, maybe that would be enough to get him through.

She stirred in his arms and snuggled into him. Snuggling her right back, he put his phone on the table beside him and tried to go back to sleep. All the while knowing, this wouldn't be enough for him, but it was what was best for her. Life under a microscope was suffocating and he wouldn't wish it on anyone. Let alone someone as wonderful as Lexi.

A few hours later he awoke to Lexi's alarm on her phone. She sat up to turn it off and the sheet fell off of her, revealing her glorious tits he hadn't had enough time with. He wanted to reach out and caress them, but that might start something there was no time to finish. So, he settled for tracing the tips of his fingers down her arm. She was so soft. He wanted to pull all that softness against him and get lost in it.

Uncertainty clouded her face as she turned to him and

pulled the blanket back up to her chest. He did not like that one bit.

"Good morning," he said as he pulled her back onto him. He wanted so badly for her to be comfortable around him, and when she nestled back in, his heart soared. He pressed a small kiss to the top of her head, and she melted into him. That was better.

"Plans for the day?" He asked, still stroking the arm she had draped across him.

"Same as every day, Pinky," she said dryly.

He sat up as much as he could without disturbing her. "Did you just quote Animaniacs?"

She laughed and buried her head in his chest. She looked up at him and the smile on her face settled in him. "I did, I must be hopelessly uncool."

"I like it... keeping it old school. And I will gladly be the Pinky to your Brain. I'll take over the world with you."

"Unfortunately, today is just work. I should already be in the shower by now, so I can eat my bagel and drink my coffee and be at work by eight. I'm kind of a creature of habit."

"I like it. Go shower and get ready for work and I will see what I can do about breakfast, but... if you had time..." he said, pulling her face to his for a kiss and sliding his hand down to squeeze her generous ass.

"As much as I would love to, I have a plumber coming to fix the sink in room three. I need to get in, but I could be persuaded to get out of there a little early, maybe show you the waterfall before we go to my brother's cookout. If you still want to do those things, of course," she added the uncertainty of finding her face again. He had a visceral need to make that uncertainty disappear, she needed to know how badly he wanted to spend time with her.

"That sounds amazing, and maybe we can sneak in some time for a quiet lunch together in my room," he said, wagging his eyebrows at her and giving her ass a little spank to make sure his meaning was not missed.

"I think that can be arranged," she said, reaching her mouth up to kiss him. "But right now, I need to go take a shower." Wrapping the blankets around her, she pulled them off the bed and made her way into the bathroom, the blankets trailing behind her. Liam was disappointed not to see her naked body as she left, but when she turned and looked at him, now fully naked and uncovered, she cocked her eyebrow. Putting his hands behind his head, he stretched out for her. Her eyes perused his body slowly and she bit her bottom lip.

"You sure we don't have time?" He asked as he stroked his cock that was already hard.

"You're not playing fair. I have to get to work. I'm already off by..." she glanced at the clock. "Oh my god, I'm off by twenty minutes and my morning routine is down to the minute. I gotta go." Then she disappeared down the hallway. Liam smiled to himself and got out of bed and started getting dressed.

After he was dressed, he headed down to the kitchen to see what she had for breakfast. Cereal boxes lined the top of the fridge, he opened it and was a little surprised at what he found. It was bare. Eggs, expired milk, shredded cheese, a long-gone bag of salad, lunch meat and condiments. He did find some bacon that looked good. Eggs and bacon it was.

Out of sheer curiosity, he opened the freezer. He found it packed with frozen dinners. This is not what he was expecting, but he needed to stop expecting things from her. She was a constant surprise at every turn. From their meeting in the diner when he had assumed she was a fan and finding out she knew next to nothing about him, and now this. At work she was the put together, no-nonsense boss, who apparently eats only Lean Cuisine.

That's it. He was going to spend the next couple days spoiling her. First, he would make sure she knew that this was only for this weekend because it had to be, but then he would spoil the hell out of her, just because he could. And he would enjoy every fucking minute of it. Right now, it was bacon and eggs. He got that going, got the coffee going and popped some toast in the toaster.

Lexi came into the kitchen right as Liam was setting the food down at the little kitchen table. He handed her a mug of coffee and pulled out her chair.

"Thank you," she said with a smile. Looking down at her plate she smiled. "This looks great. I didn't think you could have toast."

"I can't have toast, but that doesn't mean you can't," he said as he was bringing over his own plate to join her at the table. "I know we are on a time crunch. Do you need any help getting ready?"

"Nope, after we eat, I should be able to make it there only a little later than usual, but in plenty of time to beat the plumber."

As they ate, he looked around her place. It was almost like a time capsule from the early 90's, like nothing here had even changed. He hadn't had much time to look around last night, he was a little preoccupied with the dirty things he wanted to do to her. But in the light of morning, he could see this house for what it was, a museum. A worn-down museum of life in the 90's. That must have been the last time this delightful woman in front of him had anyone take care of her.

His fingers itched to start contacting people to have her

house made over. He had done a show with HGTV. He could call in some favors, but he should probably learn more about her. That was his priority today. He was going to learn as much as he could about her so he could spoil her in the best way possible.

"Ready?" she asked as she pushed back her chair and walked her plate over to the sink.

Lexi pulled up to the inn and parked in the back.

"Okay, why don't you get out and walk in and then I'll go in ten minutes? Or maybe I should go in since I'm already later than I normally am. I don't want to raise suspicion," she said looking at him with a careful look on her face.

"We don't have to do this. I'm not ashamed of spending the night with you," but as he spoke those words, he remembered what being involved meant and what being involved with him had cost his past partners. That was something he refused to put on Lexi, he wanted to make her life easier not complicate it further.

"As much as I appreciate that, and I do," she said, reaching for his hand. "I'm still the boss, you're a guest, and while there are no official rules on the books, it does seem unprofessional."

"Right, well you head in. I'll walk around and enjoy the grounds. I have some work I really should stop ignoring," he said, pulling his phone out. "But first, put your number in here."

"Why?" She asked as she tentatively took the phone from his hands.

"So I can have your contact information, in case you haven't realized I'm quite fond of you, Lexi...." he said as he tucked a lock of hair behind her ear. "I don't know your last name or if Lexi is short for anything."

"Alexis Turner," she said breathlessly, her lips parted slightly.

"Well, Alexis Turner, you better get inside before we're making out in your car at work. I'm pretty sure you would consider that to be unprofessional too," he said with a smile.

"Right." She quickly put her number in his phone and gathered her things. "Well, I'm going in. I'll see you later."

"You can count on that," he said with a smile. He barely fought the urge off to spank her round ass as she got out of the car.

As she walked inside, he stopped to collect his thoughts. What the fuck was he doing? He couldn't have a relationship with her. Not the kind she deserved. Even though it was what he wanted so badly. He wanted that very badly. He hadn't felt like this in a very long time, and that ended horribly. He wouldn't do that to someone again.

The dread of the conversation that he needed to have set in. He wanted to spend this weekend with her. Fuck her, spoil her, and then maybe they could find a way to be friends. The thought of her not being in his life regularly set a deep pit in his stomach. He knew he was someone who fell fast and hard. Feeling things deeply was all part of being an artist, but he needed to make sure they were on the same page before he proceeded any further.

He got out of the car and took a brief walk. Getting his phone out he saw her number saved there.

Liam - Can't wait to see those falls with you later *winking face emoji*

Lexi - Me either

He headed quietly back to the inn and made his way up to his room. He needed a shower and to catch up with his old manager. Part of fixing the messed-up situation he was in was putting supportive people back in his circle. His old manager Sue was just that. She had stepped aside after the last big scandal, but that was a mistake. He needed her back. That would be his first step in making things right.

Chapter 12

Lexi

Walking into the inn, Lexi tried to find some semblance of normalcy that hadn't been exploded by her night with Liam James. It was still something she was having trouble wrapping her head around. She had just spent the night with one of the most recognizable faces in the world. What planet was she even living on right now? She felt like she was floating.

"I was wondering when you were going to show up," said Nancy. "You are usually in here at eight-thirty on the nose."

"What?" Lexi said, Nancy's words pulling her out of her trance.

"Nothing, I was just commenting that you are here later than usual. Are you feeling okay?" She asked, her brow furrowed with concern.

"Oh yeah, I'm fine. Overslept. Well, I need to get to work," she said, making a bee line for her office. She needed a few minutes away from Liam to collect herself.

She collapsed into her office chair and turned on her

computer. Her mind drew a blank on what she needed to do today. Luckily, she kept a very organized calendar.

"Hey Nancy, have we heard from the plumber yet?" she called out to the front desk.

"Not yet."

Okay, she could do this. She slapped her cheeks to try and wake herself up from the Liam James dream state. It wasn't like her to get this wrapped up in a crush, or really anyone for that matter. She blew out a breath and opened her email to get to work, only for her phone to ding with a text from an unknown number.

Unknown Number - I can't wait to see the falls with you *winking face emoji*

God damn it. Now her heart was all swoony again.

Lexi - me either.

She texted back and saved the number to her phone.

Finally, after multiple cups of coffee, she had managed to find her focus. She was getting work done when the plumber showed up.

"Right this way, I'll show you to the room," she said.

After showing the plumber up to the room, she noticed it was only down the hall from Liam's. She tried not to be distracted by the thought of him on the other side of the door. As she walked past Liam's suite the door cracked open just enough to reveal a sliver of him... in a towel. He peeked his head out. When he saw there was no one in the hall he took her hand and pulled her into the room.

"What on earth are you doing?" she squealed in surprise.

"I thought I heard your voice."

"I have to get back to work..." she said, unable to take her eyes off his chest. His strong, tattooed, wet chest. He put a hand on her belly pressing her up against the door. Her heart was pounding out of her chest. She wanted badly to pull at that towel and watch it fall from his body, but she couldn't do this... not here. His mouth closed on hers and kissed her. When his tongue swept into her mouth, she could feel her heartbeat pounded in her chest. And between her legs.

Then he stopped and kept his face inches from hers "Do you really need to go back to work right now?"

She nodded, unable to speak.

"Well, I won't stop you. But I'll be down there this afternoon. You owe me a hike." He turned and walked into his room and let the towel fall revealing his perfectly sculpted ass.

"You don't play fair," she said.

"See you in a couple hours," he said without looking back.

Making her way back to her office she passed the front desk.

"Hey Nancy, let me know when the plumber is finished."

"Will do. Are you sure you're feeling okay? You look flushed."

"I'm good," she said rounding the corner into her own office.

She managed to distract herself and get some work done. Around one her phone dinged.

Liam- I'm ready whenever you are.

Lexi- I'm going to get changed and we can head off.

Liam- Don't change until I get there

Lexi- See you in a few minutes.

She quickly shut and locked her office door then changed into the spare clothes she kept there. After helping dig a car out of the mud or other mishaps that had happened over the years, she learned it was best to keep spare casual clothes. As she was finishing slipping on her jeans, there was a soft knock at the door.

"Yes," Lexi called out.

A very excited Nancy whispered from the other side of the door "Liam James is down here to see you."

"Yep, I'll be right out." She looked at herself in the small mirror that hung on her wall and smoothed her hair before grabbing the doorknob.

"Nancy, I am leading Mr. James on a hike to the falls and then I am going to show him around the town," she said as nonchalantly as possible.

"I could take him if you had work to do," said Nancy while smiling over at Liam, who was smiling right back at her.

"I can do it. I am also going to remind you that you are a happily married woman. You've been with Gus going on thirty-five years now."

"Yes, but I'm still human," she said, her eyes not leaving Liam.

"I think Lexi is going to help me scout out some spots for a video I'm hoping to film here. I appreciate your willingness to help though," he said with a smile.

"Of course," she said clearly flustered and then got back to work.

"Let's go," said Lexi. "I'm just going to drop this off in my car then we can head out."

"After you," he said, opening the door and following her out.

After dropping her stuff off they made their way to the start of the trail at the back of the property.

"So, what kind of hike are we talking about here?" he asked as they started down the wooded path.

"Not so much a hike as a leisurely walk," she said.

"Perfect, that will let me talk to you without the distraction of wanting to pull you into a bed and do what we did last night."

He took her hand once they were deeper in the woods.

"Oh yeah? talk to me about what?" She hoped she didn't sound as nervous as she suddenly was. She knew this was all too good to be true, but she at least hoped to have sex with him later tonight. If this was all a dream she didn't want to be woken up until then.

"I just wanted to tell you that my life is a mess. I don't want you to get caught up in all of it. If I lived a more normal life, I would want to date you and see where this goes, but the scrutiny I live under isn't something I'd wish on anyone. It has done a lot of damage in my past relationships and after the last time I promised myself I wouldn't date anyone seriously until I was ready to step out of the public eye. And I think that the space I've created among fans to be themselves is important--"

"Liam, that's all fine. I know this is just a weekend thing. And if you need it to be done now, I get it," she said, trying to keep her voice as even as possible.

He stopped and pulled her hand to stop her too. She turned and saw him. The look on his face was a new one she hadn't seen before. His sexy smirk, his friendly smile, even his sultry gaze were all faces she had seen before This was not one of those. It was more earnest than she had seen before. Her heart pounded in her chest seeing him like this. His star power was truly something, the magnetic draw she felt was palpable. She hoped he didn't want to finish this now.

"No, that is not what I want. I just wanted you to know that this is complicated. I wanted to be upfront with you. I didn't want to toy with your emotions or lead you on to thinking this could be something it can't be. My life just doesn't allow for it."

"I get it. I never expected more. Honestly, I never in a million years would have expected this. I would be lying if I said I wasn't drawn to you, but hey I guess that's why they pay you the big bucks, you have that star quality."

"Let's not talk about that right now. I'm just Liam with you. Liam Sheffield from Athens, Ohio. Not Liam James. Okay?"

He looked at her with eyes that sparkled, and it was all she could do to not kiss him, but they needed to get this all sorted out before that.

"Okay, Liam Sheffield. You wanna see those falls?"

"Lead the way."

They made their way down the trail to a bench that overlooked the falls. They weren't the biggest waterfalls, but they were pretty. The sound was peaceful. Lexi had spent a lot of time here when she was little. Her mom always used to take her to the falls. They would have picnics and camp in the state park. For that reason, she didn't come to the falls very much anymore. They were bittersweet. They brought good memories, but also dug up the not so good ones and the thoughts of what could have been if things hadn't gone so wrong.

"This is so beautiful! I would love to get a --" he turned and looked at her and stopped. "What's wrong?"

"Nothing," Lexi said, trying to regain her composure.

"It is clearly not nothing, I've never seen this face before, you look like you're about to cry." Stepping closer to her he rubbed her arm.

"You've known me for two days. You clearly hold infinite knowledge of the faces I make," she bit back at him. Sarcasm... defense mechanism best served ice cold.

Hurt danced across his face as his hand fell. Fuck. This is what she did. She kept people from getting to that side of her. That hurt side that had to be strong for so long, but maybe, since this wasn't real, she could let her guard down. It would feel good to let go of her hard exterior and let someone in, and it would feel safe knowing the deadline exists. He was already leaving, that was not the same as abandonment. Maybe that made no sense, but in some weird way it did.

"I'm sorry. That was rude of me." It was now or never. Be brave or explain it away. The thought of telling him without the pressure of having him in her life if things got weird helped her choose. "It's just hard sometimes to come here. I used to come here with my family. We would camp down at the camping ground and hike to the falls." He looked at her with eyes that held such a depth of kindness she felt comfortable to continue. "When I was fifteen my mom died in a car accident, it was sudden and flipped my life upside down. Seeing the falls reminds me of her... which is good... but it also makes me wonder what my life would have been like if she hadn't died."

He guided her to the bench, and they sat down. "I'm so sorry. Losing a parent that young must have been really hard." He raised his hand and wiped a tear from her cheek.

It felt good to share, so she decided to go ahead and tell him the whole story. One she had only told to a handful of people before.

"Yeah, it was hard. I was fifteen and my brother was only twelve. After she died, my dad started drinking. He was never violent, but he was sad and stopped caring. He lost his job that year. That's when I started at the inn. I was fifteen and I started coming in and doing laundry after school. That is also when my dad started to disappear. At first it was just for a few overnights, and I would get my brother and myself ready and to school in the morning. Then he started staying away for a couple days. Then that turned into staying away for a couple weeks. And finally, after over a year of that I was just done. One night, when he came back after being gone for eight days, I told him he either needed to come back for good or stay gone. When I woke up the next day he was gone, and I never saw him again." She took a shuddering breath. It felt good to say all of that out loud. "I've never told that last part to anyone, not even my brother. I think I've always felt guilty. I was so angry. I never really wanted him to leave and never come back."

That last confession did it. She had never said those words out loud before. The tears started to fall in earnest, and she found herself swept away in big emotions, grief, shame, anger. They were all there threatening to overtake her. Liam's arms wrapped around her. He held her tight, and her face found the space in the crook of his neck and shoulder, and she cried. She couldn't stop it now if she tried. And he just let her cry. He sat there holding her, rubbing her back, anchoring her to reality.

Finally gaining some composure, she sat up and wiped

her eyes. "I'm sorry. I don't know why I dumped all that on you."

"Hey," he said with a look filled with such kindness it almost broke her heart. "I'm glad you told me. I'm sorry those things happened to you. You were just a kid and that is a lot to deal with. You did the best you could."

Those words threatened to break her again. The words she had been dying to hear for so long, but no one ever said because she never told her story. Sharing herself and her story with someone like Liam felt good.

"Thank you," she managed to get out as she wiped the last few stray tears. "After all that happened, I was almost eighteen. Grace, who owns the inn, helped me to get custody of my brother. After I finished high school, I started working here full time. It has just been me and my brother for a long time. He got married a few months ago. I adore Poppy and I'm so glad that they found each other, it's just been a bit lonely since he's been gone."

They sat on the bench in silence after that, Liam's arm draped across her back, rubbing her arm. It felt so good to get that all out. After a few moments Liam leaned over and kissed her temple.

"You, Alexis Turner, are a remarkable person. I hope you know that."

She didn't have any words left in her, she just rested her head on his shoulder, and they sat on the bench looking out over the waterfall for a long time. She had no idea how much time had passed, but she was content. His fingers traced lightly up and down her arm and her hand on his knee. That connection between them pulled them together. They may just have this short weekend together, but she would make the most of it. As long as he still wanted her after the outpouring of emotion from a near stranger.

After a while her phone beeped in her pocket.

Josh- You better not back out! I will see
you in an hour at our house. Is Liam
coming?

She looked over at him and he had a small half smile on his face. It was a smaller version of the one that fills the cover of magazines, but it was still there.

"That was my brother. He was just reminding me about dinner at his place. Do you still want to go? If I didn't scare you off being an emotional mess."

"Of course, I still want to go. And you weren't an emotional mess. I still plan on spending every second with you until I have to leave on Sunday, that is if you still want to."

"Of course, I do."

She tried not to smile as big as she felt inside, but the way his own face lit up at her made her stop caring. She leaned over and kissed him. He slid his hand up into her hair and kissed her slowly. They hadn't had a kiss like this before. Their previous kisses had been passionate and surprising and new. This kiss felt different. The magic that seemed to dance between them shimmered as he sipped at her mouth kissing her with such tenderness. His mouth explored hers as if he was trying to learn her physically the same way he had just learned about her emotionally. This kiss felt like a kiss to build a lasting love with, but that wasn't what this was. He had been clear. He could only offer this weekend, and she would take it. She would take anything and everything he was willing to give.

Chapter 13

Liam

Lexi's car had just pulled up to a huge house. It was just off the town square and looked to be an old colonial house. It was white with black shutters, and it was beautiful.

"Is this your brother's house?" he asked.

"Yeah. He bought it last year. It was a whole thing. He had been saving for it because before the owners passed. It had been a big part of the town. They always held parties and haunted houses and all sorts of stuff. This corporate Airbnb place tried to swoop in and get it, and Poppy arranged this whole town event, and they ended up getting the house."

"That sounds like a Hallmark Movie," Liam said with a smile.

"You'd be surprised how much of Mystic Falls feels like a Hallmark movie."

"Are all these cars people who are here?" he asked.

"I think so. That truck is Sam's. That's Poppy's brother, he is probably here with his husband Jackson. And if I'm not mistaken, that car belongs to Hannah. She is one of Poppy's closest friends. She just moved here sometime last year with her husband Graham. But everyone here is cool, no NDAs necessary."

He smiled and shook his head, and to her surprise he leaned over and gave her a quick kiss. "Let's head in."

He wasn't quite sure what he was headed into, but it felt normal. And that was a better feeling than he could have ever realized. At the same time, there was a part of him who didn't know who to be. Liam James or Liam Sheffield. They were both good guys, but he was out of practice letting his guard down and being who he truly was. That had all been stripped away little by little with each scandal, with each magazine cover questioning his sexuality, with each time the paparazzi scared someone he cared about, with each time he pushed someone away because he wanted to protect them from scrutiny. He decided he was going to try to show up as himself. The real him.

As they walked up to the door, he squeezed her hand. She looked up at him and smirked. Liam wasn't very tall, he had dated many people taller than he was, so having her look up to him made him smile.

"What are you smiling at?" she asked as she knocked on the door.

"Just how short are you?" He asked jokingly with her. Her eyebrows drew together with disapproval, and she elbowed him.

Poppy answered the door. She was much taller than Lexi and probably had a few inches on Liam. Today her long dark hair cascaded down her back.

"Come in! Josh will be so glad you are here! Hi Liam, nice to see you again. I'll try to act like a functioning human this time. Jackson and I are in the kitchen finishing up a few things and everyone else is out back. Let me take you. Do you guys want anything to drink? We got soda and beer in the coolers out back but if you want anything else just let me know."

"It looks great Poppy, you guys have really got a lot of work done in the past couple months," Lexi said as they walked through the gorgeous old home.

"Thank you, we just finished painting the living room last week, Josh had to patch some of the plaster and the downstairs is just about done. I'll have to show you the kitchen later. He put in new counter tops a month ago, it is really coming along."

They walked out onto the back patio and Liam was overcome with nostalgia. He didn't know these people, but he had grown up with cookouts just like this. There was a game of cornhole going on in the big backyard, and Josh was manning the grill. He used to have cookouts like this with his family, his mom busy in the kitchen while his dad was at the grill and cousins playing games. He hadn't been to a cookout like this in a long time.

"Lexi!" Josh came over and gave her a hug. "I'm so glad you finally came over. Liam, welcome, grab a drink from the cooler."

"Hey, one of you come be on my team. Josh keeps leaving," called one of the voices from the yard.

"Come on, I'll introduce you," Lexi said to Liam.

They walked off the steps of the patio. "Everyone, this is Liam. This is Hannah."

A short blond woman reached out and shook his hand. "Nice to meet you. This is Graham." The towering man with red hair behind her nodded once.

"And this is Sam, Poppy's brother," said Lexi.

He reached his hand out to shake Liam's hand.

"Hey man, are you any good at bags?" he asked.

"I've been known to throw a bag or two in my day," Liam said.

"Great, you're on my team. Watch out for that one, she cheats," he said, gesturing to Hannah.

"You can't cheat at cornhole, Sam. Either you get it in the hole, or you don't. You just don't like that we beat you," she said flatly.

"Funny how you only beat me when you're keeping score."

She rolled her eyes but still smiled. "Are we going to play or what?"

"You're up," he said, tossing the bags to Liam.

Liam tossed the bag, and it slid right into the hole.

"Nice. You're going down Hannah," Sam said with a triumphant smirk.

"We'll see."

Liam looked around and Lexi was up talking to her brother at the grill. The game took place around him, the banter and the smack talk flowing. No one here had treated him like Liam James. There were no weird looks, no autographs, no awkwardness, they just let him exist. That hadn't happened for him in a long time. He relaxed into the game and meeting these new people. When he glanced up again, he caught Lexi staring at him. He winked at her, and she grinned back. Something about the perfect normalcy of this evening felt good.

"It's ready," Josh called out as he took the burgers off the grill.

They all went inside to fix their plates. "Hey, I picked up some gluten-free buns when Lexi said you might come.

Of course, there is gluten in the pasta salad, but everything else should be good," said Poppy.

"Thank you," he said, surprised people had taken him into consideration like that without his team of people.

"Of course! Let me know if you need anything else."

He nodded and waited back while everyone made their plates, opting to take it all in instead.

"Poppy, the kitchen looks amazing," Hannah said to Poppy and they both started chatting.

Sam had slipped in behind the man standing next to the refrigerator and hugged him from behind and whispered something in his ear. Lexi came and stood beside him. He wanted so badly to reach out and put his arm around her. He wanted so badly to belong to these people and this place.

"You ready?" Lexi asked him, handing him a plate.

He nodded and took the plate and filled it with all the great cookout food he could.

They all went back outside and sat around the patio table. The sun was starting to set, and Josh turned on some fairy lights. It was picturesque. This is exactly the vibe he was going for in his music video. He knew this place would give him what he was looking for.

"So, what brought you to Mystic Falls?" asked Jackson.

"It's kind of a funny story. Somehow, we ended up over a hundred miles off track and the tour bus broke down here. Then the venue for the concert we were on our way to flooded with that big storm we got the night before last. It has been an odd series of events," he said.

He noticed that Hannah and Poppy exchanged an interesting look, unsure why.

"But I decided to stay," he continued. "I'm hoping to

find a place to film the video for Home and this town has exactly the feel I'm looking for."

"Well, if you need any shots of the orchard let me know," Sam said.

"Sam, do not use this to plug the orchard," Poppy said glaring at him.

"What? I'm just saying, we have some pretty spots," he said defensively. Poppy raised an eyebrow at him.

"I'll check it out. I'm here till Sunday afternoon, then I have to head into the city. I have a show on Monday."

The rest of the night was just them around the table catching up. Lexi and Josh talked about the inn. There was small town gossip and talk of upcoming events. Lots of razzing in fun. He looked over at Lexi who was looking back. Something about this perfect night under the fairy lights tugged at his heart. If he were to ever give it all up, it would be for something like this.

As they were walking to the car with more leftovers than they could eat, he did finally take Lexi by the hand. He had been itching to touch her all night.

"I hope that wasn't too lame," she said with that uncertainty in her voice.

"That? That was amazing! I had so much fun. You have really great family and friends."

"Yeah, they're pretty great."

They got in her car, and he couldn't help himself. He leaned over and kissed her. He held her face between his hands and slowly and tenderly kissed her. He pulled back and the glazed-over look on her face made him smile.

"What was that for?" she asked breathlessly.

"Just because I can."

"Where to now?"

"Can we go back to the inn? I'll sneak you in. No one will know it's you, but I have some plans for you tonight."

"I've never stayed in the suite before."

"Then let's go."

She shook her head and huffed out a sigh. "Let's go."

His heart skipped a beat. He did have plans for her tonight. He couldn't wait.

Chapter 14

Lexi

They pulled up to the inn and Lexi parked towards the back of the lot, hoping her employees wouldn't see her car. She couldn't believe that she had let him talk her into this. They should have gone back to her house, but this was what he wanted to do, and she wanted to make him happy. They only had these few days together.

Liam had fit in so well with everyone. That made her long to have more than a weekend with him, but he had been up front. And she knew she wasn't really ready for anything serious. She wasn't sure if she ever would be. She knew she didn't want children and that seemed to be a deal breaker for lots of people. But that wasn't something she needed to worry about with Liam. This was just a weekend, a weekend that would get her through the rest of her life, the weekend she went to bed with a rock star. And honestly, that was better than anything she had previously imagined.

"Are you ready? I have experience sneaking in and out of places. Do you have any sunglasses? Oversized hat? trench coat?"

She quirked her brow. "Are you serious?"

"No, but I'm going to go with it. Why don't you go to the side door, and I'll let you in, that way you aren't going by the front desk."

"That works. It feels like high school, sneaking boys in."

"Did you sneak many boys into your room in high school?" he asked.

"Not a one," she said with a smile.

"Alright let's do this, gorgeous," he said, and he dropped a sweet kiss on her mouth. Her heart ached. This is only one weekend she reminded herself as she headed around to the side door. Watching him walk in did something to her. She still couldn't quite believe she was spending a weekend with this man. Whether he was Liam James or Liam Sheffield, she didn't care. She wanted to know more about him. She wanted to know everything about him.

Standing next to the door, she spotted him coming. He opened it quietly and took her hand and pulled her inside. She pushed down the emotion that smile evoked but held onto the lust, because as unlikely as it was, this star in front of her wanted her.

After unlocking the door, he turned to face her, his back against the door. Then turned the doorknob behind his back and pushed the door open. He turned on the light and she gasped when she saw rose petals trailing down the floor leading a path to the bed.

"What's this?" she asked.

"I wanted to spoil you for the next couple of days. I hope you cleared your calendar because you're about to get the royal treatment."

"You didn't have to go to all this trouble," she said.

"Lexi, you're worth it. You're worth all the effort and forethought. Give me just one moment."

He headed into the bathroom and Lexi looked around the room. She had been here many times before, but never like this. She had been in as the manager, as the housekeeper, but never as the guest. His guitar was sitting in the corner of the room. She walked to it and let her fingers trace over the instrument with reverence. At some points in the evening, she had almost forgotten he was who he was. He fit in so seamlessly with everyone, maybe even better than she did. But that was her own fault, she never really allowed anyone close after her dad left. It was her and Josh against the world, but Liam was breaking down the walls she had built around herself. It was scary, but it felt right. She could be with him like this before he left. She could do this.

She turned to see him coming out of the bathroom and walked over to her. Fuck. There was that lustful look in his eyes again. That look that shot straight through her and almost turned her into a puddle right on the floor. He reached for her, and she allowed herself to be pulled into his arms. He slanted his mouth over hers and kissed her.

His hands reached down as he pulled her shirt off. She tugged at his shirt, and he allowed it to be pulled right off. Then they were back on each other. They were a mess of lips and tongues and roaming hands. He kissed down her neck and she fisted her hand into his hair. His pupils were blown with lust when he pulled back and looked at her.

"Come with me," he said, pulling her into the bathroom. When she walked in the room was bathed in candlelight. There were rose petals and a bath drawn in the big, jetted bathtub that sat next to the window overlooking the falls. It was too dark to see anything, but she knew they were there.

"Candles are against inn policy," she said as she took in the room.

"It's okay," he said with a cocky grin. "I know the manager."

With that he was on her again, kissing her and unbuttoning her pants. She let her pants slip down her hips and he kicked them to the side as he undid his own. Once they were naked, she stopped to admire his body. He was doing the same to her, but then he took her hand and helped her into the tub.

"This is incredible, Liam. No one has ever done anything like this for me before."

"I'm glad to do it," he said, lowering himself into the water across from her. It was a big tub, but even as large as it was it was not all that roomy with them both in it. They sat facing each other, their backs against opposite sides. He took her foot and started massaging it. His eyes never left hers as his hands kneaded.

"So, tell me more about Liam Sheffield," she said.

"What do you want to know?"

"Well, I know you grew up in Ohio, but what else? Tell me about your family."

"I have one sister; she is still back in Ohio and is married with three kids. My mom is still there too. My dad lives in Columbus, which isn't too far. They split up when I was a kid, but they did the co-parenting thing pretty well."

His hands started massaging her calves in addition to her feet, she groaned at how good it felt. She couldn't remember the last time she'd a massage, or if she ever had. Well, that's a sad thought.

"Did you always know you wanted to be a musician?" she asked.

"Yeah, I loved performing as a kid. I would sing any chance I got. I won a local talent show at thirteen and I decided right then that singing was it for me. I left for LA when I was nineteen to try and make it, and I was just in the right place at the right time. I got an agent and a record deal when I was twenty-one and I have been singing ever since."

"How old are you?" she asked.

"I'm twenty-six."

"Really? Wow, you are a lot younger than I thought. I'm thirty-three."

"Yeah, I had to grow up pretty fast. If you don't have your head on straight this industry can really get to you. Even with your head screwed on straight, the industry can get to you." He continued to massage her leg as his hands worked higher. "But I'm all done talking about the music industry for the night, if that's okay with you," he said as his hand had migrated to the upper thigh. Her inner upper thigh. His gaze turned hungry, and she was done.

"What exactly is it you have in mind?" she asked as her breathing increased and she licked her lips. She was holding on to her last little bit of restraint, not really clear on why she was because she knew his intentions and she was ready for them.

"Well, if you must know I plan on making you fall apart in this tub. Then we're going to go to bed, and I am going to worship you until the sun comes up, if that sounds okay to you."

"Where on earth did you even come from?"

"I already told you, Athens, Ohio. Now come here." He pulled himself closer to her, water sloshing out of the tub just a little as his hands found her core. She arched her back already so needy for his touch, for the pull that wanted to be close to him. It felt like he would never be close enough. She would never have her fill.

Then she was filled by his fingers and lost any ability for coherent thought. He worked two fingers in and out of her and his thumb lightly grazed her clit. Her back arched and she found herself gripping the sides of the jetted tub as he added more pressure to her clit, and she moaned. His eyes were boring into her as he pushed her over the edge. She closed her eyes and her head fell back as the pleasure started to peek inside.

"Look at me. I want to see you."

Her eyes found him, and the waves of pleasure overtook her. His gaze held hers as he stroked every ounce of pleasure from her.

"I could watch you come forever. You're perfect."

That caused her to break eye contact. She had never been very good at accepting compliments. It wasn't that she thought anything was wrong with her. She was able to see her worth and value, she wasn't ashamed of the body society liked to shame, but still, something about compliments made her want to squirm away.

"I don't want this to sound all poor me. I know myself, I love myself and my body, but I can't, for the life of me, figure out what is going on here."

"Well, that isn't exactly what someone likes to hear after giving you an orgasm, but I get it." He leaned forward, his legs tangling with hers in the bathtub. Raising his hand out of the water he cupped her face. "I don't know what this is either, but I feel this draw to you. I want to know you; I want to know all about you. I am insanely attracted to you. In the beginning of my career, I was taken advantage of a couple times by older women, I clearly have a type." he said with a wink. "Because of those experiences, both with women and men, I learned to check for the signs of people wanting something from me or wanting to be with me for proximity to fame and the bullshit that goes with it. You don't seem interested in any of that."

"I mean I'm not gonna lie, being with a rock star is pretty amazing..." she said with a grin. At that, he grabbed her sides and tickled her, causing more water to slosh out of the tub. "Hey now! As manager of this inn, I can't allow you to make such a mess of this bathroom. You'll be charged for water damage if we don't clean this up," she said trying to hold back her giggles.

"Well, we can't have that. Let's move this to the other room." Pulling the plug, he stood, water running in rivulets down his shoulders and over the tattoos on his chest, and cock, which was mere inches from her face. She was frozen with lust. She wanted to reach out and touch him. Before she could, he stepped out of the tub, slipped into a towel, and mopped up the mess they had made. He helped her stand and then reached for one of the inn's amazing soft robes and held it open for her.

"That's not going to fit me," she said

"Just trust me," he said, helping her into the robe. Which surprisingly slid right on. As she stepped out, she tied the robe easily around her.

"Did you get one of the bigger robes? You have to request these," she said shocked.

"I told you I was going to spoil you until I have to leave, this is only part of it.... but I must admit, I am looking forward to the other part." He slipped his arms around her middle and pulled her in close. A small gasp escaped her lips as he did. His arms wound around her, holding her to him. She looked up and cupped his face, his very handsome face, trying to memorize it. The memory of these past couple days would help to get her through the lonely moments of her life.

He smiled back at her. The small smile, the Liam Sheffield smile. The one meant only for her, from the real man in front of her. It broke her heart a bit. When she got glimpses like this, it made her want to keep him here, even though it wasn't a possibility. Going up slightly on her toes, she kissed him, fisting her hand into his hair she claimed his mouth. He opened to her willingly. And there was that feeling, the magical zing that existed between them.

Breaking their kiss, he led her to the bed. She lay down as Liam went around the room lighting candles.

"Candles are still against inn policy," she said with a sultry smile.

"I'm willing to risk it." Looking at her, he pulled the edge of the towel and it dropped to the floor. She gazed at his lean, muscular build. Tattoos covered his shoulders and chest, down his stomach to his cock which was already hard. "Are you ready?"

"Get over here," she said.

He crawled up the bed until he was kneeling before her. Her robe was still loosely tied shut and he pulled at the belt. Opening it he looked at her with a look that was almost reverent. "You are so beautiful, Lexi. I hope you know that."

Slipping her arms from the robe, she ran her hands over her breasts and bit her lower lip. At the moment he lost whatever ounce of control he was holding onto and pounced on her. Good. She wanted him to be as lost with lust as she was. Pressing her into the mattress, he kissed her. This kiss was a lust drunk mess of teeth and lips and tongues spurred on by pure desire. His hands explored her body, roaming over all the hills and valleys, paying special attention to her breasts. He started kissing down her neck and massaged her breast, plucking the nipple to a peak. His mouth found the other nipple, licking and sucking as he went. She moaned and arched her back when he bit down. The shock of that little pinch rippled through her body.

"Liam, please," she begged.

"Please what?"

"Please, I need you inside of me, right now."

Reaching over into the drawer beside the bed he pulled out a condom. He ripped it open with his teeth and then rolled it down his cock. His hands slipped over her thighs and between her folds. Filling her with his finger, she cried out. He swept up until his finger found the sensitive bud and swirled around it. She was embarrassingly close to coming just from that contact, then suddenly he pulled his hand away and laid over her, positioning his cock at her entrance. Pushing in he filled her, and she clung to his back. Even though her slippery core offered little resistance, the stretch she felt as he slid in made her whimper.

"You feel amazing," he said as he rocked inside of her. He kissed her mouth, her jaw, her ears and her neck. She began to move with him. He changed his position, so he was more upright, then he put his hand in the crook of her knees and pushed them up. He continued to move, his eyes watching where their bodies met.

Lexi moved her hand down her body and started to rub her clit while he moved inside of her. His eyebrow cocked, still gazing at their connection. He hit that spot deep inside of her and she cried out. Her fingers worked faster as he began to fuck her in earnest. He was no longer gently rocking into her; he was picking up speed and fucking her hard as he hit that spot over and over.

She saw stars behind her eyes as her entire body pulsed with pleasure. Her hand had fallen away but he was still there chasing his own desire. Then he stiffened and gave two last thrusts before grunting and collapsing on top of her. They both lie there sweaty and panting trying to come back to each other. Pulling out, he kissed her. It was the sweetest barely there kiss in comparison to what they had just done. It pulled at her heart that was already dangerously close to caring too much for this man.

He excused himself and went to the bathroom to clean up and take care of the condom. She then went to the bathroom. When she came back, he was laid back on his bed, still naked strumming on his guitar. Fuck. She was done for.

Chapter 15

Liam

Their eyes locked as she stood there in the doorway of the bathroom. Her robe was tied loosely round her, her hair looked a mess, and the flush of her orgasm lingered on her cheeks. In that moment, he wished things could be different. If he could be here with her and still be who he needed to be for his fans and for everyone who depended on him as Liam James, he would do it, no matter how hard it was. He was so fucking drawn to this woman standing before him. It was nothing he had ever experienced before.

Yes, he had been in love before, many times. Liam loved love. It was part of what made him such a good artist, those emotions lived right under the surface. It was easy to be overtaken by them, but he also got to get lost in the good ones. And right now, looking at this woman he didn't want to fight the wave of love that was coming, but he knew she deserved better than the life he could give her right now. She deserved more than living in the fishbowl of public scrutiny, and that was all he had to offer. But fuck... if ever there was a person, he would give it all up for, she would be it.

He stopped strumming his guitar and patted the bed next to him.

"What are you playing?" She asked.

"I'm just messing around. You have my creative juices flowing," he said. She had no idea how long those creative juices had been gone and the fact that he could feel a song coming was like manna from heaven. And it was all thanks to this connection.

"Me?"

"Yes, Lexi, you. You're incredible. It's like I somehow was meant to come here and find you. And now I don't want to leave." She made her way over to the bed. "Are you tired?" he asked.

"Not at all, but I should probably go," she said with an uncertain look on her face. Was it possible she still didn't understand just how much he craved her, how much he needed to be near her?

"Not a chance, I told you I had you for the night. And spoiling takes many forms." He pulled back the covers and she hopped under them. He stood, slipped on some boxers, and grabbed a bag from the corner. "I didn't know your preferred movie snack, so I got it all," he said as he dumped out a bag of candies and chips and all kinds of goodies onto the bed.

"What is all of this?" She asked, grinning up at him.

"Snacks. You need to build your strength back up. I'm not done with you tonight." he said as he flopped down on the bed next to her the treats jumped in front of her and she reached out and grabbed a bag of Twizzlers. "Twizzlers, a wise choice," he said, reaching for the remote. "What do you want to watch?" he asked.

"Do we have to watch anything?" she asked as she opened the Twizzlers.

"I suppose not, what would you like to do?"

"If I only get such a limited amount of time with you, I want to talk to you. Learn more about you... if you want to."

"Of course. Tell me something about you," he said as he opened a small package of gluten-free Oreos.

"Hmmmm. I won the county spelling bee in sixth grade."

"Nice. I can't spell for shit," he said with a chuckle.

"What about you? Tell me something about you no one else knows. A bit of you I don't have to share when you leave."

Those words dug into his heart. He didn't want to leave, but he pushed them away, for another time.

"I used to get dressed up in my mom's sequin vest when I was younger and sing Shania Twain. Okay, well that might not count because now I do that for millions of people," he said as he twisted apart his Oreo. "Okay, how about this, when I was in the seventh grade, I led a walk out in Biology because of the inhumane treatment of frogs."

"Did you really?" She asked as her face lit up. He nodded. "So did I!" she said with a chuckle.

"Wait, what? Are you serious?" he asked.

"Yep, I led half the class out and I got detention," she said, ripping off another bite of her Twizzler with her teeth.

"I got a Saturday detention and I had to do a virtual lab," he said, nodding his head in agreement. "I know we were destined to meet."

"Broken down bus," she said.

"Broken down bus hundreds of miles off track," he corrected. "Still need to get to the bottom of that one."

"Whatever the reason, I'll take it," she said as she

reached her face up to his for a quick kiss. "You're kinda cute."

"Can I ask you something more serious?" he asked, twisting apart another Oreo.

"Of course."

"So, I know you almost googled me and then stopped, did you ever follow through with that?"

"Nope, it just kind of feels like a weird invasion of privacy. If there was some public source of information about me, I know I would rather people hear things right from me. No spin."

"I know after I leave, you might be tempted. I just want to tell you something, so you can hear it from me first."

"Okay," she said, sounding a little unsure.

"The last relationship I was in was over two years ago. He was the bassist from my touring band. There was one night we were at a club in Vegas. We were young and drunk and in love. Long story short, I gave him a blow job in an elevator, because why the fuck not, and I didn't even stop to think about cameras. Somehow the footage fell into the wrong hands. Luckily the label was able to kill it, but plenty of pictures of us being drunk and handsy in the club will come up. The publicity got really bad. He decided that all of this wasn't worth it. He left the band and left me... and really, I couldn't blame him for it. It was a massive violation of privacy. My whole life seems to be a massive violation of privacy."

His gaze left hers. He hated this. He didn't feel ashamed of who he was or who he loved, and this wasn't even really about that. It was about that everyone felt entitled to him. Everyone felt entitled to every aspect of his life. And while he knew that was all part of the gig, sometimes it was just too much. Then he felt her hand on his knee. It was like an anchor, holding him here to this moment, to this woman, and it was everything.

"So, yes," he continued. "If you google me, you will see all kinds of pictures of me making out in Vegas, all kinds of articles questioning my sexuality. All kinds of people asking very personal questions that they don't have a right to ask just because I make music for them. That is why I decided after everything happened there that I couldn't be in another relationship until I was ready to call it quits. I can manage this life, but I don't expect anyone else to put up with it. It's just not worth it."

There was a long pause while she rubbed small circles on his leg waiting for him to finish. Eventually she cleared her throat.

"That's shitty," she said plainly.

He gave a rough chuckle and swept his hand through his hair. "You can say that again."

"It's shitty," she said. "That's not fair to you, Liam. You deserve love and if you find someone willing to figure it out with you, I hope you let them. You spend so much time making everyone happy. I just hope you can find someone that makes you happy."

"Even if I could find them, which is hard to do, how could I ask someone to take on that burden?"

"Because you're worth it."

She said it so simply, like it was easy to believe. Like the heaviness of his life was something he could get help with from another. He wanted that, craved it. Yes, he loved sex. He was very open with his body and his attraction. But this, what was happening right now, was something he hadn't experienced before. The level of connection and intimacy he felt in this moment was more than he'd ever felt.

He gave a weak nod to her words, not certain he agreed.

"Hey," she moved his face until their eyes met. "You are worth it. If you find someone who you connect with and they are willing to push everything aside, I hope you let them."

"Would you welcome all of this into your life? Paparazzi? Public Opinion? More NDAs? Who in their right mind would want those things?"

"I can't answer that right now. I'd need to think about it. But I can definitely say I think you're worth it. And I think if you really thought someone was worth it, you should let them make that decision."

Those words gave him way more hope than he should let himself have, but it was there, nonetheless. Maybe they could figure something out, but the crushing weight of the what ifs and the fear of causing someone else pain wasn't a fair fight for that weak glimmer of hope.

He leaned over and pressed a kiss to her lips. "Well, you let me know if you think it's worth it, because you're the first person I've connected with in a long time."

He said it as a joke, but it wasn't. The words lingered there in the air. He couldn't take it anymore. "Tell me your most embarrassing moment," he said, popping another cookie into his mouth.

And the night went on like that. They laughed and shared secrets. Then they fell into bed shortly after midnight and made love again and again. The last time he looked at the clock it was three. He had Lexi wrapped in his arms holding her soft body to his. Soon after he drifted off to sleep.

The next morning, he woke up and the sun was already streaming through the windows. Lexi was still there in his bed snuggled into him giving soft snores. It was so fucking cute. He looked at the clock and saw that it was already after nine. Holy fuck, he hadn't slept for more than a handful of hours in longer than he cared to remember. He snuggled her one last time then rolled himself away from her. Quietly, he called down to room service and ordered almost everything on the menu that morning so she could have her pick.

He wasn't ready for this to be over. They had one more night together, but he was hoping he could turn it into two if she was interested. He slid back into bed with her, and she snuggled into him. They fit so perfectly, and he wasn't sure how or why they had ended up together like this, but he was so thankful. He didn't want it to end.

Chapter 16

Lexi

There was a knock at the door and Lexi woke up. It took her a moment to realize where she was. She was in the inn with Liam James snuggled behind her.

"Room service."

"Be right there," Liam called as he swept her hair from her face and pressed a kiss to her temple. "Morning gorgeous, do you want breakfast?"

She sat up and pulled the blankets around her, she was still naked from the night before. Liam went to the door and kept it as closed as he could so they couldn't see in.

"Did you order the whole menu?" she asked with a yawn.

"I just wanted to make sure you had your favorite. Let's see what we have." He began lifting the lids off of plates. "We have an omelet, French toast, eggs Benedict, blueberry pancakes, a veggie frittata, and of course toast with an assortment of jams."

"Blueberry Pancakes!" she said immediately.

"You got it," he said, bringing her the pancakes and cup of coffee. "Cream sugar?"

"Nope, black is good for me," she said, taking the plate from him. He got himself a cup of tea, grabbed the veggie frittata for himself, and joined her back in bed.

"I must say, this inn is top notch," she quipped.

He grinned at her. "Here's a little secret, I'm sleeping with the manager, so we get the good stuff."

"You get the good stuff everywhere you go," Lexi said with a cocked eyebrow.

"Not like I do here. I get some special services while I'm here," he said as he leaned over and kissed her. How is it possible that after everything that's happened over the past day and a half, a kiss and a smile still made her heart skip a beat?

"So, you're a tea drinker?" She asked, sipping her coffee.

"Yeah. I recorded my last album in London, and I have great appreciation for English breakfast tea. Unfortunately, finding a good cup over here isn't that easy. Sometimes I think about flying over there just for another cup."

"You would fly across the ocean for a cup of tea?"

"Well not just for a cup of tea, but yeah, why not?"

"Must be nice..." she said.

"It is. I know that I am at the peak of privilege, but I try not to let it go to my head," he said in a tone she hadn't heard before.

"I didn't mean anything by it, I just can't fathom that," she said, watching him as he took a bite looking out the window. "Ya know when I first saw you, I wasn't sure what to think. Then all the stuff with your manager and the NDA, I thought you were this out of touch spoiled rock star. But now I don't think that at all."

He looked at her, emotion dancing behind his eyes and

she wanted to know what he was thinking, because right now she had no clue.

"What do you think of me now?" He asked with a look that pinned her in place.

"I think there's more to you than what everyone sees. I see a person who cares deeply about his fans and the people around him. I see a selfless person who gives up things he wants because he worries his life will cause others pain. I see a person who has so much love to give but doesn't have a place for that to go so he spends it on his fans, on his work, on his family, on spoiling random women," she said with a wink, "but he doesn't prioritize his own happiness."

He looked at her for a long moment, his eyes welling up with tears. He blinked them away, but she saw them. She saw him.

"Do you want to know what I see when I look at you?" he asked.

Did she want to know? She didn't feel like she knew the answer herself anymore.

"I see someone who cares about those around her and works her ass off without taking any time for herself. I see someone who put herself on the back burner for so long that she has trouble separating and seeing her own wants and needs. I see someone with the weight of the world on her shoulders. And instead of letting all that turn her into a person full of resentment, I see someone who still chooses kindness and sees the best in people. I see you."

He leaned in and kissed her. How is it possible that someone she had known for about forty-eight hours could see into her soul this way? See that part she had hidden away to protect when life got too hard.

"You should come to London with me sometime. I would love to show it to you."

"London... Wow, I never thought going to London would be a possibility for me."

"Where have you traveled before?" he asked.

"Not far..." she said.

"How far?" he asked.

"Well, I've been to New York City a couple times on a class trip. My mom took us to Niagara Falls when I was younger, but that's it."

"You've never left New York State?" he asked.

"Nope. I would love to see more of the world, but I just never had the capacity."

"Come to the city with me," he blurted out.

"What?"

"Come to New York with me. I can spoil you much better in the city."

She narrowed her gaze. "What are you talking about? You were very clear on what you could offer. I have this one weekend with you. That doesn't include a trip to the city, I'm not some charity case."

He looked at her mouth slack, eyes wide. "Charity case? Where the fuck did you get that idea?"

"I just don't want you doing these things for me because you feel bad for me."

"I want to bring you because the thought of you being far away from me physically hurts me. I still can't promise much and maybe this is a bad idea, but I don't know if I care right now. Come with me, I can get us into my building without being seen. You can come to my concert Monday, and we can have one last night together. I want you with me because I am selfish and I want you, not because you're some fucking charity case. So, lose that thought right now."

"You're serious?"

"Yeah, I'll have a car come and pick us up right now and take us into the city."

"I have to work on Monday," she said.

"I have a feeling you have some vacation days stored up."

And she did. She never took time off. Maybe she could do this. She knew Nancy could handle things.

"Okay," she said quietly.

"Yes?" he asked, joy dancing behind his eyes.

"Yes, let's do it."

"Yes!" He said as he pulled her into his arms and kissed her. Then kept kissing her. He laid back and pulled her on top of him. She sat up straddling him, all the sudden very aware that she was still naked under this robe, and he was only wearing boxers. Desire shot straight through her as she rocked on his already stiffening cock. Looking up at her he cocked his eyebrow and pulled at the belt of her robe. "I like where your mind is, gorgeous," he growled, taking her breast into his hand and she arched under his touch. He pulled her down for a kiss and somehow managed to wiggle down his boxers and slip on a condom. Then she rode him until they both climaxed and lay next to each other panting.

"Okay, here's what we are going to do. First, we are going to take full advantage of that shower, then you are going to go home and pack. I'm going to clean up here and call a car. Then I'll come and get you and whisk you away for two nights in the city."

"That sounds amazing."

"Good," he said, dropping a quick kiss on her mouth. "Now let's get in that shower."

Chapter 17

Lexi

Lexi was relieved she managed to make it to her car without being seen. She made her way home still floating in the clouds. How was this her life? This is only for the weekend, she told herself over and over. The hope of more simmered beneath the surface when she was with him, but when she stepped away, she could turn the heat off.

She unlocked her door and went inside. Something about it felt normal, which made the absurdity of the last couple days come into contrast to her normal life, which was full of frozen dinners and repeat episodes of New Girl.

It was a life that she didn't hate, but was it fulfilling? That was a dangerous question to ask. She had given up so much to take care of Josh. College, relationships, all of that. Josh came first. She didn't regret that, and she didn't resent him for it. He didn't ask for a tragic accident to take his mother and alcohol to slowly take his father any more than she had, but he was younger. He had needed her to be strong. He had needed her to hold it all together so he wouldn't get put in the system. So that's what she had done.

She had pushed it all down. She had done the work and lived her life for the two of them.

Now Josh was married and happy. And while Lexi was so happy for him, she didn't know how to search for her own joy. She didn't know how to sit still long enough to find out what she truly wanted. She worried if she sat still and listened to herself, the ghosts of her past she had never dealt with would pop up and leave her playing whack-a-mole with her trauma. Abandonment and fear and grief all lived just under the surface, threatening to pull her down if she ever stopped for too long. So, she had kept moving, kept working, kept on living a life on autopilot. It didn't leave much room for joy, but she survived, and truth be told she was pretty proud of that. But was being proud of her strength enough for her? After these two days she was beginning to doubt that, but those were thoughts for another day.

Maybe this wasn't a good idea. Maybe going to New York with him would only make it harder to get back to her real life. Maybe this was all a big mistake.

Her phone beeped in her purse and pulled her out of her thoughts. It was a text from Liam, along with four missed texts.

> Liam- ETA 40 minutes, don't back out now. No rethinking things while I'm away. I'll be there to get you and take you to the city whether you like it or not *winking face emoji*

How could he read her mind even when they weren't together?

Opening all her texts, she saw one from work, she would deal with that one when she called Nancy about being out Monday. The rest were, of course, from Josh and Poppy

> Josh - So what's up with you and this rock star guy?

> Josh - He seems ok, but I just wanted to check in with you.

Of course, he did, because Josh looked out for her just as much as she looked out for him these days.

> Poppy - OMG LIAM JAMES! You have to tell me everything ASAP!

Lexi chuckled and opened her contacts to call Josh. She needed to tell her brother she was leaving town. If he came here looking for her and couldn't find her, he would spiral.

He picked up on the second ring.

"Lexi?" He always sounded slightly panicked when he wasn't expecting her to call.

"Hey Josh, I just wanted to tell you I am going to the city for the next couple nights."

There was a pause.

"Josh..."

"You're going to New York? With Liam?"

"Yeah. I'm going to go to his concert on Monday then I'll be home on Tuesday."

"What is going on with you two?" he asked with barely veiled suspicion.

"What do you mean? I was just showing him around town for his video and then he offered to take me to his concert as a thank you."

Another pause.

"What?" Lexi asked, losing her patience.

"I don't know, you were just different around him. And the way he was looking at you..."

"Josh, he is a superstar. He can make anyone feel like that. It's part of being adored by millions."

"Poppy told me to have you ask him if he knows Bridget," said Josh.

"Bridget who?"

"Bridget... I don't actually know her last name. But the woman who owns the magic shop in town."

"Why on earth would I do that? And how would he possibly know her?"

"I asked Poppy the same thing, but she just told me to trust her... and that woman's intuition is on point almost all the time."

"Okay, I'll ask him. Anyway, I'm leaving shortly and just wanted to tell you so you wouldn't worry. I'll call you when I get home."

"Sounds good. Have a safe trip, love you."

"Love you too." She hung up and started to pack. What she had to wear that was concert appropriate she didn't know, but she was off to see.

She opened her closet door and looked at her small assortment of clothes. There was one outfit she could wear, so she pulled that out and then dug into the back of her closet for her bag. She really had to dig. It had been a long time since she had needed her overnight bag, but that wasn't a surprise.

After she packed, she noticed there were dishes in the kitchen sink. Those would need to be done before she could leave. And honestly it would give her something to do. Otherwise, she would second guess things again.

As she was finishing up the dishes there was a knock at her door. She dried her hands and went to open it. Even knowing who it was didn't stop the butterflies in her stomach from fluttering around when she opened the door to a smiling Liam James.

"Hey gorgeous, Are you ready?"

"Just about, I just have to finish up the last couple dishes," she said, heading back into the kitchen.

"Can I help?"

"I'm basically done, but would you mind heading upstairs to get my bag?"

"Of course." As he walked through the kitchen, he stopped and put his hand on the small of her back and gave her a little kiss. That small contact pulled at her heart.

"What's this?" he asked as he came down the stairs.

She was drying off the last plate and slipping in into the cupboard when she looked to see Liam holding a large poster board. He flipped it around and Lexi's heart almost stopped. It was her dream board. The last one she had ever made.

"Where did you find that?" she asked.

"It was on the floor next to your closet," he said as he set her bag on the floor and gazed at the posterboard.

"It must have fallen out when I was getting out my bag. It's a dream board I made when I was fifteen. My mom and I would make one every year on New Year's Day before she died. That was the last one I ever made."

Looking at this was surreal; she hadn't seen it in a long time. She couldn't even really remember the person who had made this. There was a corner with big NYU letters and a picture of a Rolling Stone cover. She had wanted to be a music journalist, well she had wanted to be an MTV V-jay, but this seemed more real to her teenage self. The rest were places she wanted to travel. The Eiffel Tower, Big Ben, The Pyramids, and, of course, her fifteen-year-old Twiheart self had included Forks, Washington in hopes of meeting Robert Pattinson. There was even a picture of Robert Pattinson eating sushi. Did she add that for him or the sushi? She had never had either one of them come to think of it.

"Wow, I haven't thought about this in years," she took a deep breath. This was not something she could deal with right now. She was feeling a little off balance from the last couple days, and something like this could easily pull her down. "Well, I'm all finished up. Let's get out of here."

"Have you ever done any of these things?" he asked, his eyes still taking in the board.

"I haven't had the chance," she said, trying to make light of the situation because this was not a road she could go down right now.

"Not even sushi with Robert Pattinson?"

"Sadly, no sushi or Robert Pattinson."

"Well, they're both delightful," he said, smiling back at her.

"Good to know. Let's get going."

He picked up her bag and they headed out the door.

<h1 style="text-align:center">Chapter 18</h1>

<hr>

<h2 style="text-align:center">Lexi</h2>

The ride to the city had been far different from her previous experiences, which had required a school bus. This time, it was in a sleek black car with tinted windows and a separating panel that Liam had taken full advantage of. Having an orgasm while barreling down the highway courtesy of Liam's talented fingers was definitely different, but she assumed she was in for lots of new things over the next day and a half.

When his car had pulled into a below ground parking deck she kept her eyes peeled. After they got out she stood by the trunk to get her bag out. Liam took her hand and reminded her that someone would bring the bags up. He walked right into the elevator, pushed in the code, and they rode up to the penthouse.

When the elevators opened she took in the space. It was huge. One side of the room had floor to ceiling windows with an amazing view of the city. Everything was sleek and modern, but still had touches of Liam Sheffield scattered around. There was a rainbow throw blanket on the sleek leather sofa, and a framed picture on the wall that she assumed was his family.

"So this is it. When I'm not touring, or recording an album, this is where I stay," Liam said as they entered. "The whole top floor is mine. Plus a couple guest suites and apartments for my team."

"Wow, this is amazing," she said. "So your manager's here?"

He nodded. "Well, she might not be here, but if she's in the city, she stays here."

"She's probably got that NDA already, just itching for me to sign it," she said, joking with him.

"Well, I'll have to tell her to add in a clause about all the stuff I told you willingly. Her head would explode if she knew I told you about the elevator video. I think that whole fiasco is why I was 'persuaded' to hire her. She's the daughter of one of the lawyers from my label. He was the one that got the video killed, and I think this might be their way of keeping an eye on me, like I'm some sort of deviant who goes around giving everyone blow jobs in an elevator. Which even if I was, who fucking cares? The label fucking cares I guess."

There was an edge in his voice she hadn't heard yet. Maybe he enjoyed their time in Mystic Falls as much as she had and this was an unwelcome return to his reality. Maybe he would regret bringing her here. Walking over to him, she slipped her arms around his waist and leaned her head on his shoulder. He slid his arms around her and held her tightly and kissed her temple and sighed.

"Come on, let me show you around."

He led her around the space. There was a huge kitchen, media room, and a small personal recording studio.

"Now this is the room I spend most of my time in," he said as he came to a door in a long hallway.

Lexi was preparing herself for his bedroom, tingles of excitement filled her. She was about to see the room 'where the magic happens' as the saying goes. But when he opened the door, it wasn't what she was expecting. This was his music room. There were guitars on the wall, a giant piano in the middle of the room, an overstuffed comfy couch and chair, and a bookcase filled with books. On the other side of the room was a giant cork board, tacked up were pictures of his family and friends, and letters. So many letters.

Upon closer investigation, she saw they were fan letters. Letters thanking him for giving them the space and the words to be who they truly are. For giving them the courage to dress how they wanted to dress. For being able to finally come out to their parents. For his music that got them through dark times and changed their lives. This was what he was talking about. This was why he gave so much of himself away that there were only scraps left for himself.

Seeing these letters and this room clicked something into place for her. She had felt like she knew him in a way that didn't make sense. She had felt like she understood him, but she couldn't be sure. But after seeing this room, she didn't doubt that anymore. She knew him. And knowing him kind of broke her heart. She wanted to protect him. Help him to save more than these little pieces of himself. He deserved more than little pieces of himself.

When she looked over at him, he was rubbing the back of his neck with a far of look in his eyes. She smiled at him warmly and he smiled back, but it didn't reach his eyes.

"Are you okay?" She asked.

"Yeah, I'm fine," he said, putting his hands on her hips

and pulling her to him. "I don't normally bring people in here."

She put her hands on his chest, his heart was pounding, matching hers. "Thank you for showing it to me. This room holds the most of you."

"It does," he said in a voice barely audible and pressed a kiss to her temple. "I haven't spent much time here lately. It reminds me that I haven't written a song in over a year. I haven't gone that long since I started writing songs at fifteen. I'm just blocked," he said with a deep sigh. He nuzzled her head and pulled her close.

"I think there's one room we haven't seen yet," she said, looking up at him.

"There is. Follow me." Taking her hand, he led her to the door at the end of the hall. He opened the door, and it almost took her breath away. It was another room with floor to ceiling windows. There was a fireplace with a seating area the size of her whole living room. In the corner she saw a bathroom that looked incredibly indulgent. She was hoping she would get to try it out. On the back wall was an amazing giant four post bed. It was the bed of her dreams. The pillows were big and full; pillows just asking to be snuggled. The fluffy blankets looked so soft she couldn't wait to touch them.

She wanted to rumple this bed right now. Wanted him to pound her into the mattress until it was just the two of them and nothing else existed. She wanted to lie in it for days with him and shut out the rest of the world, their only care in the world being their next orgasm. Her ability to have these thoughts surprised her. Even more surprising was the length she would go to make them a reality.

Walking across the room, she traced her hands along the

bed. She was right, these blankets were so soft. He joined her next to the bed and sat down. "What do you think?"

"This is amazing. Do I get to sleep in this bed with you?"

"I'm hoping you'll do more than sleep in it with me," he said, pulling her between his legs. His hands rested on the generous swells of her ass as he pulled her closer. Seeing him in his space centered this in reality. He was no longer some magical force that showed up in her little town. Here she saw the weight of his life. The weight Liam James put on Liam Sheffield, and she wanted to lighten the burden. That wasn't her job, but maybe over these next couple nights, she could try.

She pulled his face up and kissed him. They had had their handful of kisses that felt important, and this was one of them. The first kiss after she put together the pieces of this man. The shininess had worn off of Liam James and she could see who he really was. She kissed him slowly, pouring everything she could safely give into him.

He stopped kissing her and she felt him grin against her mouth. He leaned back and pulled her onto the bed on top of him. Then, with some skillful moves, he moved them closer to the center of the bed. He now kneeled over her, his thighs bracketing her. His hands held her wrists above her head and his face was mere inches from her own. A small gasp escaped her mouth.

"Hi," she said, unsure of what else to do.

"Hi." He kissed her and she tried not to lose herself completely to this magical moment.

"Liam, where are you?" a female voice called from the hallway. He rested his forehead against hers and groaned. He moved to get off of her when his door opened.

"Oh, it's you!" said a voice she now recognized as Jacinda, his lovely manager.

"Jesus Jacinda, knocking is a thing!" he said to her, resentment dripping from his voice.

"Meet me in the living room. We have some things to go over before tomorrow." She closed the door and left. His brow was furrowed and he got off of Lexi and ran his hand through his hair.

"I'm sorry about that. I shouldn't have given her the codes. I'll be right back." He turned and left the room, shutting the door loudly behind him.

She had never seen him that angry. He had every right to be angry at someone storming in on them, but it was still just another facet unlocked. With each newly discovered piece of him came a fierce feeling of protectiveness. She wanted to march out there, not to make a scene, but to let him know someone was on his side. Not the side of Liam James, but the side of him that existed between the two

But she didn't move. She just sat here on the bed, unsure of what to do next. Being alone made her think about her reality. She needed to text Josh and let him know she arrived safely, but didn't know where their bags were. She looked at the clock and saw it was four. They still had tonight, but their time together was falling like sand through the hourglass. She hoped Jacinda wouldn't keep him long.

After about fifteen minutes he came back looking tired.

"I'm sorry about that, she won't storm in again. I may even fire her after this tour. I've been talking to my old agent. She was with me in the beginning and is the only person I really trust." He blew out a breath.

"Okay. Here's the plan. We'll order take out and spend the night together with no interruptions. Tomorrow at noon I have to be at the venue for a sound check. Then I have some pre-show things I need to do, but those can be done here. I can guarantee privacy if you want to come with me to all the concert stuff, but you can stay here if you prefer. That's up to you."

"You have nothing to apologize for. I'm happy for any time I get with you. I do need to text my brother and let him know I got here safely. I would also love to freshen up. Do you know where our bags are?"

"Oh, of course. They're in the hallway. I'll grab them, that is if you've decided on staying in here with me tonight," he said, knowing damn well she intended on staying in that bed with him.

"Ok, bring the bags in."

Then he smacked her on the ass and left. She smirked. Something so casual and normal felt good.

Chapter 19

Liam

As he came back, he couldn't help but smile. It felt good having her in his space. She fit here with him. He could see a future with her. She had managed to make him feel more like himself than he had in ages. Something about her practicality and not being swayed by Liam James made him trust her in a way he hadn't trusted anyone in years. They just understood each other. The level of trust that normally came with years of building, came in a matter of days. It shouldn't be possible, but it was as true as anything he had known.

"Did you text your brother?" he asked.

"Yep," she said, setting it on one of the chairs.

"I think it's awesome you guys are so close. I haven't talked to my sister in a few weeks, even though she emailed me a few days ago. I need to call her to make plans for my nephew's birthday, but I have been a little preoccupied."

"Oh," she said quickly. "Go right ahead. I can step out."

"I think it can wait. Right now, I just want to snuggle you on this bed," he said as he patted the space next to him.

She made her way to the bed. "As much as I have

enjoyed my time with you, I think I may enjoy my time in this bed more."

"You wound me." He pulled her down next to him. He loved the way her soft body formed to his. She laid beside him, her leg draped over his and her breasts pushing into his side. Her head resting on her hand that was on his chest. With that warm smile on her face, something about her felt like home. He'd experienced instant attraction before, but it never involved this much intimacy.

"How long have you lived here?" she asked.

"I bought this place a couple years ago. Sadly, I don't think I've stayed in it more than a week at a time before."

"Really?"

"Yeah, I usually go home in my off time. The city has never really felt like home. I think I like the idea of the city more than the city itself. If I lived someplace like Mystic Falls, I think I would try and spend more time there. As nice as this is, it feels empty. But," he said, pulling himself away from her, "it does allow me to spoil you a little better." He went to his closet and brought out a gift bag.

"What's this?" she said. Her face looked almost painful. He could have guessed she would be someone who didn't like extravagant gifts, but that was too bad. He was an amazing gift giver.

"Only one way to find out," he said, gesturing to the bag in front of her.

She reached in and pulled out a jewelry box. She looked up at him, eyes wide. "You did not have to do this."

"You don't even know what I did yet."

She opened the box and her eyes softened. It was a charm bracelet, Nothing extravagant, just beautifully senti-mental. Even Lexi would have to agree with that.

"Liam, this is incredible. I don't know what to say," she said with tears in her eyes.

The bracelet that had already had four charms. One Silver letter L, one storm cloud, one guitar, and a water drop. He gently took her hand and put the bracelet on her wrist. "The L is self-explanatory. The cloud and the guitar are from that night on the porch swing, which was the first night I wanted to kiss you. The water drop is for the waterfall, where you shared your story with me." His fingers traced along the charms and along her wrist, he pressed a kiss there and continued to hold it.

The emotion in her eyes when he looked up was enough to take his breath away. "Liam, no one has ever gotten me anything like this before. I don't think I can accept this."

"It is for you, personalized from our time together. Take it so you can remember this weekend."

Her hand cradled his face, and he felt his heart breaking. One weekend with this woman would never be enough. He should have known. But he had her now, and he was going to take full advantage of it.

"When did you have time to do this?" she asked as she admired the bracelet.

"I called Heinrich, my butler. He ordered it from a store I frequent, and they brought it over, and I had him put it in my closet. I think we should figure out what you want for dinner. We can do anything: sushi, Italian, fancy New York food at its finest or pizza and ice cream if that's what you prefer."

"I've never had sushi before," she said quietly, "I don't know if I would like it."

"Would you like to try it?"

"But if I don't like it, then it would be wasteful. Let's do something else."

"Would you like to try sushi?" he asked again in a firm tone.

She nodded.

"Sushi it is," he said confidently. He wasn't sure why the thought of doing this for her made him so happy, but it did. He dug his phone out of his pocket and texted Heinrich to get them sushi.

"While we wait, I want to spoil you in another way. Personally, it is my favorite way," he said as he kissed her neck.

She gave an agreeable hum.

"I'm going to need you naked to do what I am intending to do to you," he said as he reached for the hem of her shirt.

"Only if you lose your clothes too."

Getting up on his knees he peeled off his shirt and may have flexed his abs while doing so. He'd done enough shirt-less shoots by now to know how to look his best. Her slight gasp as her fingers traced his taut stomach showed it had the intended effect. He stripped off her shirt, his mouth on her neck and chest. She reached around and undid the clasp of her bra and slid it down her shoulders. He squeezed her breast and licked her nipple, then drew it into his mouth. They each attempted to remove their bottoms, but it quickly turned into a mess of lips and tongue and teeth. Trying to devour each other as they lost their clothes. He planned this to be a leisurely round of oral sex, but this was escalating.

He finally managed to slide his pants off and pushed her back on the bed where he yanked her pants down. Then he kissed down her chest, stopping briefly to pay attention to her breasts on his way to his destination. He kept going lower over the mound of her belly until he was kneeling between her legs. He pushed them wide and licked his lips. Pleasuring women like this had always been something he enjoyed doing immensely, but he was fairly certain that he had never seen a pussy quite as perfect as hers.

Running his finger down her seam, she was already so wet. She squirmed at his touch as he pushed in a finger and spread the slickness around her clit. Soon he sunk that finger deep inside, then adding a second. She gasped and rocked into his touch, spearing herself on his fingers and grinding on him. He began to pump his fingers in and out, looking for that special spot. She moaned and he knew he had found it. Then he licked her with the flat of his tongue from her entrance all the way back up to her clit with delicious slowness. Her hand fisted into his hair, and he began to lick little circles around her clit.

The hand fisted in his hair tightened and her breathing became short little pants, she was almost there. He had wanted to draw this out more, but he couldn't help himself. He sucked that little bundle of nerves, and she broke. She cried out and he was there licking her and working her through each wave of pleasure until it subsided.

When she was done, he moved back up and pulled her to him. As her heartbeat returned to normal, it matched his. He liked that. He kissed her sweat-dampened temple.

"That was incredible. Your mouth is talented in so many ways," she said. He kissed her sweetly and ran his hand through her shoulder-length blond hair. Sitting here gazing into her blue eyes something was changing inside of him, and he knew if she asked him to, he would try to make things work. That was a scary thought, but it was true. If she wanted to, he would move heaven and earth to make this work. Whatever this was blossoming between them, was something truly special, and something he didn't know if he would ever experience again.

"What is it? You have a look on your face."

Nothing got by her. She was one of those people so attuned to the feelings of those around her. That was possibly why she was so good at working at an inn and why she had been such a good person to take care of her brother, but he wanted desperately to take care of her. To be the one who looked out for her and put her first. He wasn't sure if anyone had done that for a long time.

"I was just thinking about how much I've enjoyed my time with you. How grateful I am for the bus to have broken down. And how much I don't want this to end."

Please say it doesn't have to. Please say you want to make this work. He didn't even know what that would look like, but he knew he wanted it. Wasn't she the one who said he was worth it? Even if he still wasn't too sure of that fact himself. Was it a good idea? Probably not. Would that stop him from trying even if it should? No. And that was a new revelation. Revelations made during oral sex had to be good revelations, right? But she said nothing.

She finally spoke. "Have you noticed our heart beats match again?"

"I actually did. It must be a sign."

"A sign we are often too horny around each other," she said, grinning up at him.

"I think you may be onto something." With that he took a condom out of his bedside table and winked at her.

After another all-too-satisfying romp, they laid there together. Liam's phone dinged on the bedside table, and he reached over to get it.

Heinrich - Your dinner is ready, sir.

Liam - Thanks

"Are you hungry?" he asked.

"Very."

"Well let's go eat."

"Ok, let me go clean up." She got off the bed and headed into his bathroom. He thought of her in there. His thoughts wandered to the massive shower he had in there... with a bench... and multiple nozzles... That definitely had some inspiration for later.

She came back out in comfy pants and a hoodie. "Do I need to get fancy to eat dinner?" She asked.

"No, you look perfect. You look delicious. You look like we should never leave this room."

"Let's go eat."

Chapter 20

Lexi

They moved to the dining room. She couldn't keep her eyes off Liam. Even just in a pair of sweatpants he looked like a star. She wanted to be near him. She wanted to touch him. She wanted so much she didn't really know what to do with all of it.

Turning the corner, the table was full of sushi. Like, *full* of sushi, enough sushi to feed a family of five. Next to the sushi was a big cheese pizza.

"What is all of this?"

"I didn't know what kind of sushi you like--"

"So, you ordered the whole menu?"

"No," he drew out. "I ordered the most popular items."

"And the pizza?"

"In case you don't like the sushi."

"This is too much! What are we going to do with all the leftovers?"

"I'll give whatever we don't eat to the team. Pizza and sushi will go fast, trust me. Now, what do you want to try? The California Roll is probably the safest, followed by spicy tuna. It looks like we have some unagi, tempura rolls, and some sashimi. You might want to try the rolls first, but please, try whatever you want."

She loaded some rolls onto her plate, and he did the same. There was so much food she didn't really know what to do. She watched Liam put a little bit of wasabi on his roll before popping it into his mouth.

Lexi did the same, but she put a bigger glob of the green stuff on and popped it in her mouth.

"Wait!" Liam protested.

But it was too late. The sushi roll along with a big glob of wasabi was already in her mouth. Immediately her mouth was on fire. The heat shot right up into her sinus and made her eyes water. She reached for the glass of water in front of her and started chugging it.

Liam gave a small chuckle and rubbed her leg under the table. "Sorry, I should've told you, a little wasabi goes a long way."

Her eyes were watering and the heat in her sinuses started to dissipate.

"Wow, you can say that again."

"Here," he said, taking his chopsticks and placing a small amount of wasabi on the roll before offering it to her. She opened her mouth, and he fed her the sushi roll. "Better?"

She nodded as she chewed. It was really good. She hadn't had much seafood because Josh wasn't a fan, and Josh had done all their cooking, hence the Lean Cuisine life she led now.

"Now, I'm no Robert Pattinson, but what do you think?" he asked.

"It's really good. As much as I would like a sparkly vampire here, you'll do," she said, adding another piece of sushi to her plate. Now that she knew her wasabi limit, she ate a couple more pieces.

"Hey, I'm sparkly," he said with a pouty lip. "I'm not sure what's in his closet, but if it's sparkles you want, trust me, you want me over Robert Pattinson any day."

"You're right, you're much better than my teenage crush." She leaned in for a quick kiss.

He hummed into her kiss. "And don't you forget it."

After a few more pieces, Lexi laid her chopsticks on her plate. "That was delicious."

"I'm so glad you liked it. I wish I could take you out, maybe go dancing. Or something a bit cheesier like a carriage ride around the park. I wish I could do more."

"You are doing enough, more than enough."

Eating sushi shouldn't make her emotional. Sharing a meal with a handsome superstar shouldn't make her emotional either, but here she was trying to swallow back tears. There was so much she had never experienced. The dream board he found kept creeping into her mind. She had so many dreams when she was younger. Her life was fine, she had survived, but it had been a long time since she thought about that little girl and all her hopes and dreams.

"Then why do you look like you are about to cry?" he asked gently as his hand reached up to wipe a tear that had slipped out.

"I don't know. Being here and eating sushi after seeing that board just reminds me of all the things, I never got a chance to do. Things like college and being young and irresponsible were things I never got to experience. I can at least check sushi off that list now. It really does mean a lot to me. No one has ever done anything like this for me. I'm still fairly convinced I'm going to wake up and this will all have been a dream, but I'll have a newfound love for the pop sensation Liam James."

"Well, I can definitely say you're not dreaming, but I do hope you wake up with a newfound love for Liam James."

"Oh, trust me, I have a love for Liam James, and a growing fondness for Liam Sheffield."

An expression clouded his face, one she hadn't quite yet figured out. She wanted to know what that meant. She wanted to know what all of his expressions meant. But he had made it clear, this was for the weekend. That was it. So, she would cherish every single moment she could with him. Every. Single. Moment.

"Come with me, I want to show you something. It is part of the reason I bought this place."

Taking her hand, he shut off the lights and led her to the windows. The view of the city at night was breathtaking. All the buildings were tall and lit up with little squares. She had seen pictures like this in the past, but here in person, it was even better than she thought it would have been.

Looking at the millions of little squares of light that lit up the buildings, she thought about the people in them. What were they doing? What kind of lives did they lead? Whatever they were doing, she knew there was no way they were as happy as she was right now. He slid behind her and his arms wrapped around her waist. Resting her hands on his, she leaned back into him.

"This view is amazing," Lexi sighed contentedly.

"It is. I love the city lit up at night. Looking at all those little squares of light, imagining the people there and what their lives must be like."

She turned in his arms and looked at him.

"What?" he asked.

"I was just thinking that. About the people and the squares of light. Like literally just thinking about it. Are you psychic? Do you have mind reading capabilities you haven't let me know about, because I think this is unfair if that's the case. I guess it would also explain this whole thing."

"Not a mind reader, but great minds do think alike."

"You can say that again." She turned in his arms back to look at the skyline again.

"This whole conversation reminded me. Poppy asked me to ask you the most ridiculous question but knowing Poppy she will expect an answer."

"Shoot."

"Ok, so this is random, but just go with it."

"Now I'm intrigued. Proceed," he said nuzzling into her ear.

"So, there's this little old woman in Mystic Falls. She runs a magic store. Tarot readings, crystals, the whole bit. Anyway, Poppy is convinced the witch works love spells and told me to ask you if you knew Bridget."

"Bridget who?" He had gone very still, but his arms were still around her.

"I don't know her last name, but she is Scottish and short and has this wild red hair with a gray streak."

"I think I do know who you're talking about. At least I ran into a woman who fits that description named Bridget at a music festival a few months ago. She was there reading tarot and selling stuff, people there loved it. I paid her to come back to my trailer and read my cards. And I actually ran into her the morning my bus broke down in Mystic Falls."

Lexi stepped fully out of his hold and turned to look at him. "You're serious?"

He just nodded and looked at her perplexed.

"Do you really believe in that stuff?" Lexi, trying not to show her own skepticism.

"Yeah. I've seen so much weird stuff over the years. Stuff

I can't explain, so I just stopped trying to explain it. I think there are some mysteries that we will never have answers to. Women like Bridget are one of those things I learned to trust a long time ago."

She just looked at him. Although being here in his space did make him real to her, there still was something completely unreal about their situation. Magic would be an easy answer, but she didn't know if she actually believed it.

"I'm just saying our bus broke down over a hundred miles off course. That storm that we watched on the porch when I first wanted to kiss you was the same storm that flooded the venue, giving me these couple days to spend with you. I mean, it seems like there are definitely some unexplained forces at work here."

"You might be right," she said. While that wasn't something she was willing to believe, at least not fully.

Before she knew what had happened, his mouth crashed into hers in a deep kiss. She lost herself in lust. Following him to his bedroom he made quick work of their clothes, and they were once again naked in his bed. Maybe there was some magic at work because he was right, nothing else made sense.

Back in his room, they made love again and again. She didn't know it could feel this way. Nothing compared to Liam, his mouth, his hands, his body, anyway he wanted her. He was taking care of her. That wasn't something she was used to, but she liked it. She drifted off to sleep in his arms, still half afraid she would wake to find this was all a dream.

She woke up in the middle of the night and rolled over to snuggle into Liam only to find a cold, empty space where she thought he would be. Checking her phone, it was three-thirty. What on earth was he doing? Then she heard the piano music drifting through the wall behind her. He was in his music room. She hadn't really watched him play except for those few moments in the hotel room when he absent-mindedly strummed the guitar. She got out of bed, pulled her pajamas on, and went to find him.

Her bare feet padded down the hallway to his music room. It was cracked and she just stood there listening to him play. She was transfixed. He was so talented. Hoping she wasn't intruding on a private creative process, she slowly pushed the door open, half expecting him to tell her to leave. But instead, he looked up at her, his eyes connecting with her pinning her in place.

He patted the piano bench next to him and scooted down a bit. Walking into his space she couldn't help but feel like she was entering somewhere holy. Where he took all the world and all the pressure and turned it into music that meant so much to so many people. She sat next to him as his fingers played the keys as if they moved on their own. But she knew this music came from a place deep inside of him that he selflessly shared with the world, and he was now sharing with her.

"So, I've been thinking..." he said. His voice sounded small, nervous, not like his normal confidence. She waited patiently for him to continue. "I know I said I could only give you one weekend, but I don't think I can leave it there."

Taking his hands off the keys, he turned to fully look at her. "I've never felt like this about anyone, and I've only known you for a few days. I promised myself I wouldn't get into a serious relationship until I was ready to be done, and I'm not ready to be done yet, but I don't think I can walk away from you. It would take more strength than I have to give this up, as selfish as it might be. We should have a serious discussion. Life can get really complicated under public scrutiny. You don't have to say anything right--"

"Yes!" she said quickly, only slightly embarrassed she had just proclaimed that so loudly. But she had wanted this since their first date.

"Are you serious?" he asked.

She nodded and tried to will away the tears that she felt burning in her sinuses. He grabbed her face and kissed her. The pull that had existed between them from the very beginning was so strong now it was palpable, like a physical force pulling them together. When they touched, the energy that rushed through her lit up every nerve in her body. She couldn't explain what was happening with Liam or why, but it was there all the same. Knowing it wasn't ending was all that mattered right now.

"We really do need to have a talk about what that means. I need to share with you the truth of what being with me would be like. Then, if you're still willing to try, we'll figure out something that works for both of us. My traveling and your job, it is a lot to put on a new relationship, but I think it is worth it."

"I do too. Can you play me a song?"

He looked at her and winked. "That's what I do."

He began to play and softly sing, and she turned into a puddle right there on the bench beside him. She was gone. Hopelessly in love with a man she had known a handful of days.

While she sat there on the bench with him a big yawn escaped her mouth.

"You should go back to bed. Tomorrow is going to be a big day," he said as he lightly traced her jaw.

"It's a big day for you too. I just have to watch you perform, you're the one that'll be doing all the work."

"I know. You'll find I don't sleep much."

"What do you mean? We all need sleep, and I'd think you do especially."

"I'm not disagreeing with you; I'm just saying I have a terrible time sleeping. I do my best work at night. My most creative juices flow at night. Plus, the day keeps me busy with all the other stuff."

"Okay, well why don't you come and lay in bed with me. Maybe I can help you fall asleep."

"Let's go, but before we do, I wanted to talk about something. We're going to see where this goes, right?"

Just hearing those words again made her light up deep inside. "Yeah, we are."

"So, tomorrow I think you should come to the sound check, and the radio interviews I have before the concert. Get a chance to see what all this is really like. To see if you even think I'm worth all the trouble."

He said that without a hint of joking in his voice. Did he seriously think his job would make her change her mind? If so, he had no idea how far gone she already was.

She turned her body more to his on the bench and cupped his face in her hands. The smile on his face was enough to melt her heart. She wanted to scream from the rooftops how much she loved this man. While they weren't there yet, she wanted him to understand how much he meant to her.

"I would love to go with you tomorrow. I look forward to seeing you perform and everything else you do, but I can guarantee you that I'm ready for whatever comes my way, if I get a shot to be with you."

"You can't say that yet... You don't know what it's like."

"That's true, I don't. But I still know that beyond a shadow of a doubt, you are worth it." And after sharing that undeniable truth with him, there was nothing left to do but make him believe it. She kissed him and tried to pour herself into the kiss and let him know how much he was worth. Because even if it was a giant pain in the ass, he was worth all of it.

Chapter 21

Liam

Liam woke to a knock on his door. He grabbed blindly for his phone to check the time. It was eight-thirty. He had slept another five hours after their late-night conversation. Lexi was going to be good for his sleep. He had already slept more in the past three days than he had in the previous three weeks. This was a very welcome change among the other obvious perks of having her around. The fondness he felt for her was deepening. He wanted to label that deep fondness differently, but he wasn't ready to go there yet.

The knock sounded again, even and non-urgent, meaning it couldn't be Jacinda. Extricating his arm from under a sleeping Lexi he took special care not to wake her. If this was something they were going to do, he wanted her to be well rested for the day.

He pulled on a robe on the way to the door. When he opened it, Heinrich was standing there. "Sorry to disturb you, sir. Ms. Moore is adamant about speaking with you."

"It's fine, I need to talk to her anyway. Can you get breakfast going while I talk to her?"

"Of course, sir. What would you like the cook to prepare?"

"Ummm." He thought about Lexi, still asleep in the bed. "Tell her I have company and to make something special."

"Right away." Heinrich turned and made his way down the hall. Liam found his discarded sweatpants and t-shirt and slipped them on to go find Jacinda. The thought of firing her was running through his head with more frequency. After all the NDA stuff, the way she had treated him and spoken about and to Lexi really bothered him.

He hated that part of being in charge. Firing people was something he'd never done, but it just might be time. Jacinda came on right after the scandal. He thought Jacinda's protection of him was out of wanting to make his life easier, but he was starting to think that it may be more about the bottom line. He was a commodity and not a person, that thought did not sit well with him.

As he turned the corner, light was pouring in from the windows. It was an overcast rainy day, perfect day for lounging around, playing music and hanging out with Lexi. But those thoughts were doused at the sight of Jacinda on the couch. She was on her phone. The terse expression on her face told Liam all he needed to know, and he was ready to turn around and go back to bed, but at that moment she turned. "Oh good, you're here."

"I'm here," he said, flopping into the chair next to the couch.

"We need to go over today's schedule. As of right now you have a sound check at twelve, an interview at two, another online interview at two-thirty and, of course, the show tonight. I went ahead and scheduled a meeting with the label to discuss the next album. We are still trying to solidify the concert that needed to be rescheduled, but after that we can book studio time. You seem to work your best when you are away. We did London last album, where were you thinking this time?"

"Wait. I don't know if I'm ready for the next album yet."

"That's why we need to meet with the execs. Get some ideas and logistics figured out," she said while looking at her phone the entire time.

"That's not how this all works, I'm not a performing monkey. I have a process."

The look on her face was comparable to the day he sent her away from the inn. She wasn't used to him asserting himself, but it was time he started. He needed to be back in the driver's seat of his career again.

"I'll be ready for sound check, and I'll do the interviews, but that's it for today," he said firmly.

"What am I supposed to tell the label?" she asked indignantly.

"You can tell them you didn't clear it with me and I'm not available."

"But you are available. I keep your schedule," she said.

"No, I am not available. I'm going to spend the morning with Lexi before we go to the venue."

"We go to the venue? Who's we?" she asked, eyeing him suspiciously.

"Well, the team, me, and Lexi."

"She is going to sound check with you?" she asked, mouth gaping.

A rage started simmering somewhere deep inside of him. Letting other people take the lead on his career had been easier when he was in a bad place, but things had gotten out of hand.

"Yes. She is. And she will be at the interviews with me. She'll have a special area to see the show and she'll spend pre and post show with me. She will be taken care of and shown an excellent time. Am I clear?" he paused and glared at her. "In fact, why don't you just steer clear of her all together." Taking back that control felt good. He would, of course, take that kind of control for Lexi. He wanted her around, and he didn't want to see her get hurt.

Jacinda's mouth fell open and she scoffed at him.

"We're finished. We'll be ready for the car at eleven-thirty. Just tell Heinrich to let us know when it's available. Email me the schedule and who I'm interviewing with. I can take it from there. You can see yourself out." He got up and headed back down the hallway. He had a cute girl in his bed to check on.

The simmering rage in him was new, and while it wasn't his favorite emotion, he at least felt something. He hadn't felt much of anything in a while. He had thought it was a good sign that he was over the heartache. He didn't realize the lack of emotion had left a haze.

His last album an introspective into heartbreak and finding your community in a world that doesn't understand you. It resonated with so many people, but he hadn't written since then. He didn't want to meet with the label today, but even if he did, he would have nothing to say. But as the fog was lifting, he realized that's how they preferred it. They preferred him docile and broken, and he wasn't that anymore. In fact, sitting at the piano last night before had Lexi come was the first time he had felt his creativity coming back. After this tour he needed some time off.

Quietly, he opened his bedroom door. It was still dark because of the blinds, but they needed to get a jump on the day. But then he saw her, still curled up under the covers. A new, deep contentment filled him all the way down to his fucking toes. He slowly climbed in bed with her. He pulled the remote out of his bedside drawer and pushed the button. The blinds slowly slid up revealing the rainy city skyline. Maybe he should have Heinrich bring them breakfast in bed. He was in no hurry to leave her.

As the light filled the room, Lexi stirred but didn't wake. She snuggled into his side, and he wrapped his arm around her. He would definitely be texting Heinrich to bring them breakfast in bed. He held her, gazing at her face. How was it even possible that someone he hadn't even known a week had become so special to him? There really was something magical at play here. Then he remembered Lexi had mentioned that woman who had read his tarot. She had talked about an unexpected love coming into his life and turning it upside down. She had also told him that he needed to be careful who he surrounded himself with, but those seemed pretty stereotypical things to say to a rock star who often found himself in the rumor mill.

Whatever made it happen didn't matter. All that mattered to him right now was this woman in his bed. She was the force pulling him and driving him to take back control, and she didn't even know it.

As he watched her, her eyes blinked open. Her eyes were still cloudy with sleep, but her smile was clear, and it was for him.

"Good morning, beautiful," he said as he swept the hair away from her face and pressed a sweet kiss to her temple.

She yawned and stretched. "What time is it?"

"It's almost nine. I have breakfast coming soon." Her fingers absentmindedly traced the sparrow on his chest. "Then we'll get ready for the day, unless you thought better of it in your sleep and now want to take it all back." He was joking, but there was a small part of him that believed she would come to her senses and decide she wanted no part of his life.

"Not even a little. In fact, quite the opposite." The press of her breast into his side shot straight to his dick. He raised a knee to hide the erection that was about to start tenting the sheets.

"I had the strangest dream," she said with a yawn.

"Oh really? Now you have my attention."

"I can't tell you. You'll think I'm some sort of stalker fan." Her face turned into his chest, hiding her eyes from his gaze.

"Considering you can't even name three of my songs, I'm pretty sure I won't think that."

"Okay, but when you want to run away from me, just remember you asked for it. You also promised I could see your show tonight, so no going back on our deal."

"Deal. Now tell me about this dream. Bonus points if it's dirty."

"Nope, not dirty. We were living in Mystic Falls at the Founder's Day celebration. We ran into Bridget, and she seemed to know all about us and said something cheeky about the bus breaking down. I got the distinct impression she set this all up. Anyway, that was about it.... feel free to run. I know you don't want to live in Mystic Falls with me."

"Who says I don't?" he said jokingly, but there was an undercurrent of truth that was unexpected. He did like the idea of living in Mystic Falls. He felt more at home there than he had here in the city, and the paparazzi likely wouldn't venture to a town that small very often. The moment hung between them, neither of them speaking.

A gentle knock sounded at the door, breaking the silence. "Come in," Liam called out.

Heinrich entered with a cart full of plates. There was a big bowl of fruit and a basket of toast. "Thanks, Heinrich."

"Of course, sir. Will there be anything else? There is tea and coffee on the tray along with your smoothie, Mr. James. If you require anything else, I can get it for you."

Liam looked over at Lexi and raised his eyebrows waiting to see if she needed anything else.

"This looks amazing, thank you. Coffee is great."

Heinrich nodded and exited the room, softly shutting the door behind him.

"Breakfast in bed two days in a row. You really are spoiling me. Going back to cereal and coffee before I run out the door to work is going to be a rude awakening," Lexi said, giving another big stretch. Liam was tempted to say he would find a way to keep spoiling her, but he wasn't sure what things would look like after this weekend. Sure, she had agreed last night to see where this went, but surely that didn't mean it would change her day-to-day life that early. As much as he wanted to keep her right here next to him always, she had a life in Mystic Falls. He couldn't keep her from that.

"Let's see what we have." He got out and lifted the lids. There was scrambled eggs, French toast, and an assortment of breakfast meats. "See anything you like?"

"Mmmm I'll take french toast and bacon." He handed her the plate of french toast and took the eggs for himself. "Just the eggs?" she asked.

"And don't forget this fruity chalky concoction," he said holding up the green smoothie. "On show night, I tend to eat lots of protein to keep my energy up."

"I'm really excited to see you perform." she said.

He was excited too. He hoped she would see his world and be able to see a place for herself in it. Having her by his side in all of this would make things considerably less lonely. He was now becoming aware of just how lonely he had been recently. Partly because of his own doing, but he was beginning to think it was also by design.

They finished up their breakfast and got ready for the car to come. He was nervous. Not for the show, he knew how to do that, but because she would be there. He needed to make sure she was comfortable and felt safe, but he also needed her to see a future with him. The need threatened to overtake him if he thought too much about it. So, he tried to let it go and mentally prepare for the show.

Chapter 22

Lexi

Lexi sat in the first row of the balcony along with some music industry people and contest winners. It was the best seat in the house for sure. Sound check was fascinating. Learning all the behind-the-scenes stuff was really eye-opening. Watching Liam interact with his band and practice a few numbers was amazing. The interviews had been fun too, although it threw her off a little to watch him be the charming Liam James for interviews. It reminded her of their first couple meetings when he was this famous rock star and she was... well, she was a bumbling idiot.

But somewhere over the course of their week together, he had dropped the shiny exterior of Liam James he was in the interview and became Liam Sheffield. She liked him better like that, although that larger-than-life smile of his and the panty melting wink got her every time. No wonder he was the object of so many people's fantasies. She had made a few of her own watching him like that.

But watching him live in concert was like nothing she could have imagined. He was electric. He was running all around the stage, dancing, reading his fans signs, and talking to them. During one of his songs, the entire place was singing along with him, and a giant conga line formed down on the floor. The floor was a sea of pride rainbows and boas and handmade signs. This was more than she could have imagined. He was captivating. And yes, she knew he could sing, but seeing him perform from the depth of his soul was something else altogether. No wonder people loved coming to his shows. He came alive out there on the stage.

There were a couple times she had caught him searching for her in the crowd. When their eyes had met and he smiled the megawatt smile up at her, she almost melted. She didn't know what he was like after shows, or what his energy level would be like, but she was so fucking turned on. She really hoped that performing made him as horny as it made her. Because damn.

Looking out over the crowd she had a feeling she wasn't the only person that was incredibly turned on by him, but knowing she was the only person who got to share a bed with him tonight felt incredible.

When it was time for him to perform Home, the song he had told her he was most proud of and meant the most to his fans, she could tell why. This song was all about unconditional acceptance and love in a world that doesn't always love you back. It was about finding and making your own family when the family you have has turned you away. Watching him perform this song with tears in his eyes to a crowd of people who were so moved deepened her understanding of it. One fan in the front row was having a particularly hard time, and Lexi watched as Liam's eyes connected with her. He mouthed "Are you okay?" Lexi couldn't see her face, but she nodded, and Liam gave her a wink and a thumbs up. He somehow managed to make everyone in this arena feel connected to him, even the ones in the back row.

This song is why he does it. She understood that now after seeing him perform better than she could have before.

After the last encore the energy in the building was buzzing. He was amazing. As people started exiting the venue, she looked around. She had no idea where she was supposed to go when it was all over. A woman in black pants and a black t-shirt with a headset approached her. "Are you Lexi?" she asked.

"That's me."

"Great, follow me. I'm taking you to Mr. James' dressing room."

She couldn't follow this woman fast enough. She wanted to get to him right away. It was official. She was now the leader of the Liam James fan club.

She was led back into the room they had been in before the show. It was a huge dressing room. There were two chairs and a big couch along with a wall of mirrors with the big round bulbs above them. Liam was already there, standing with his back to her, chugging a bottle of water. He looked like a fucking god. A fucking god she wanted to ride until all the orgasms had been wrung from her body and she was just a puddle of fulfilled desire on the floor.

The door shut behind her and Liam turned around, zeroing in on her. His gaze was hungry, and she felt it right between her legs. He moved with purpose and shoved her against the door. His mouth came crashing down on her. His hands were everywhere, and she gripped his back, trying to catch her breath.

"I need you, right now," he gasped out as his mouth kissed down her neck.

"Yes," she panted.

"Stop me if I do anything you don't like or I'm too rough, but I have to have you right here." He locked the door behind her and kissed her hard. "Tell me you'll stop me if you want to. No questions asked."

"I will."

"Good." He tugged her pants down and moved her toward the counter. In one swoop he cleared it. "Up," he said, helping her onto the counter. He pulled her ass right to the edge and lifted one leg over his shoulder. She was already wet from watching the show, but he didn't waste any time. He spread her open and licked her with the flat of his tongue from the entrance to her clit. She moaned in surprise at the suddenness of all of it. That only seemed to spur him on. He sank two fingers inside of her as his tongue circled her clit. Holy fuck! This was not going to take long. Then he kept his pace, fucking her with his fingers and licking her clit. Her hand grabbed at his sweat-slicked hair, and she fisted it in her hand, grinding hard against him.

A low guttural sound came from him, and his fingers picked up pace as he sucked her clit into his mouth. That was all it took. She was coming hard, and he wasn't letting up. He was there still eating her and fucking her with his fingers. The build inside of her intensified. When she thought she couldn't take anymore, another orgasm ripped through her. He finally stopped and looked up at her from his kneeling position on the floor and wiped his mouth. Just like that, she was ready for another round. Which was good, because the look on his face let her know he wasn't finished with her yet.

He pulled her off the counter, removed her shirt, and moved her over to the couch. She landed with a huff and his eyes were still burning right through her. He undid the button on the high-waisted trousers he had been wearing and pushed them down, kneeling before her again. He pulled a condom from somewhere and rolled it on. Pulling her ass to the edge and her legs around his waist, he thrust into her in one go. She cried out again. He didn't take his time. He thrusted into her with strength and speed that had usually taken a while to build to.

Another orgasm was building inside of her, and she couldn't believe there was still more want and need for this man. She would never have her fill of him. He fell on her and kissed her neck. Somehow his fingers undid her bra, then his mouth was on her breasts, sucking a nipple firmly into his mouth. She began grinding against him harder. Slipping a hand between them he began to rub her clit. Between the sucking and the fucking and now those fingers, she broke again, sobbing out yet another orgasm. He slowed, his eyes on her, still thrusting.

Once he helped her ride the waves of her orgasm, he slid out of her, his cock still hard and erect. He turned her around and placed her hands on the back of the couch. Bending her over, he licked her from clit to ass, then plunged deep inside of her. She let out a guttural cry as he fucked her into the couch, one hand on the back of the couch next to her the other on her ass. He pounded into her, his thumb holding a firm pressure over her asshole. She hadn't done anything there before, but with how good it felt, she wanted to try it soon. She felt another climax building in her. He pushed his knee against hers until she was kneeling on the couch, her knees now wide apart., He reangled and hit that spot over and over and over. That sent her once more. She was probably screaming, but she couldn't be bothered with that right now. Nothing else mattered.

He moved both of his hands and gripped her ass, his fingertips digging in. They would leave marks. Good. She wanted to be marked by this man. She wanted proof of what happened in this room because she would never be the same again. He thrust into her two final times and went stiff. She could feel his cock pulsing deep inside. He collapsed onto her back, covering her with kisses as he tried to catch his breath. He pulled out of her and discarded the condom in the trash.

He collapsed on the couch and pulled her onto his lap. She flopped onto him, unable to support her own weight.

"Holy fuck..." she panted.

"I'll say," he panted back at her, peppering her with kisses.

Once she started to come down from the high, she looked at him. He was still fully dressed with his pants just under his hips, and she was bare ass naked sitting on a couch in a dressing room having just been fucked within an inch of her life. She chuckled quietly to herself.

"What's funny?" He asked.

"Sometimes I still can't believe this is real life."

"I hope that was okay. Did I hurt you?" he asked, eyes full of concern.

"Maybe a little... but it was so hot. I was so turned on watching you perform. I was hoping something would happen, but that was beyond anything I could have imagined."

"Good. There is a high that exists on stage. When I saw you a couple times during the show, this was all I could think about."

"Well, I'll have to see more of your concerts. We've had good sex, but I think we leveled up there."

He pressed another kiss to her sweaty temple. "You're good for my ego, you know that."

There was a firm knock at the door. "Liam, the execs are here to talk to you."

He buried his face in Lexi's still naked and sweaty shoulder. "Fuck" he groaned. He lifted his head and called over the back of the couch, "I told you I wasn't meeting with them today."

"You told me you were meeting with them this morning. Why is the door locked?" She asked as she jiggled the handle.

"For privacy. Fuck Jacinda, I'm done for the day. I'm not meeting with them tonight or tomorrow. They can all fuck right off for all I care."

"They're not going to be happy," she warned.

"I don't really care. Is the car ready? I want to go home," he said.

"Why are we having this conversation through a door?" She jiggled the handle again.

"That's a very good question, Jacinda, as far as I'm concerned this conversation is over. We'll be out for the car as soon as I'm changed."

"What do you want me to tell them?" she asked indignantly.

"Tell them whatever the fuck you want. This conversation is over."

He got up off the couch and went into the bathroom. She heard the shower turn on. Lexi was left there, unsure of what to do. She had just had the most transcending sexual experience of her life, and now she was cold and alone on a random couch.

"Liam.... Liam... Fuck!" Footsteps stomped away from the door.

Lexi got up off the couch. She wobbled a bit but steadied herself on the arm, then gathered her clothes.

After some time passed, she was dressed just waiting on the couch. For what? She didn't know. Things felt off, and she wasn't sure why. She pulled her phone from her purse and checked the time. It was right after midnight. She only had a little while left with Liam and this is not how she wanted to end things. There was a message from her brother.

> Josh- I hope you are enjoying your weekend in the city with your rock star.

She just tucked her phone back into her purse and waited for Liam.

Chapter 23

Liam

The warm water streamed down over Liam's body as he soaped his hair. What the fuck just happened? He'd had the most mind-blowing sex with a woman he was almost certain he was in love with, only to be interrupted by Jacinda. And what the hell was up with her? She had never been this pushy before. He took a deep breath as he rinsed his hair, trying to get his temper under control.

He realized he left Lexi out there, alone on the couch. At least he hoped she was still there. This was not how he wanted this to happen.

Tomorrow, when Lexi was in a car headed back to Mystic Falls, he was firing Jacinda. Then he didn't know what was next, but he knew he needed to take back control. Spending some more time with Lexi in Mystic Falls was just what he wanted, if she still wanted him after everything. But if the sex they just had was any hint, then she still seemed to be fully on board.

He got out of the shower and pulled on some clothes,

then headed out. His heart almost stopped when he saw her sitting there. She looked like she was one step from bolting out of the door. In that instant he knew he couldn't be without her. If their week together had taught him anything it was how much he needed her in his life.

"Are you okay?" he asked gently as he sat down beside by her.

When she looked over at him a soft smile found her face and he started to relax a bit.

"Yeah, I'm fine. I wasn't sure what to do, if I should stay or go." The uncertain look in her eyes broke his heart. She should know that she belonged by his side. It was his fault she didn't. He took her face in his hands and pressed a soft kiss to her lips. She sighed and relaxed a little more.

"Of course, you should have stayed. You belong with me, wherever I am. If that's still where you want to be." He gazed at her like she was something precious, her face still in his hands.

"Okay," she said.

An actual smile crept across her face, and he took a breath. "I apologize for that. My emotions were still all over the place and that incident with Jacinda kind of sent me over the edge, but that's all it was. I'm firing her tomorrow after you leave."

"You don't have to fire her on my account," she insisted.

"I'm firing her on *my* account. I had no clue how much control she had taken over. I let her do it after everything with Henry, but I can't do that anymore."

His eyes scanned the room. The makeup table was a mess and the couch had been moved a good twelve inches out of place. "We sure did a number on the room, huh?"

At that she broke into laughter. He laughed with her. It was that kind of cleansing laughter, where your sides hurt, and it pushed out all the worry. That is exactly what he had needed to feel after tonight.

"Let's go home," he said as he stood and offered her his hand.

"Let's go."

The stage was already halfway broken down and his roadies were packing it up. He had one more show and he would be done with this tour and ready for a break.

He led her to the spot where the car would pick them up. He leaned against the cool wall and pulled her close to him. They kissed softly until the car came and took them home.

What existed between them was special. He only hoped she felt it too, because to him it was becoming a sacred truth. She was becoming his North Star. While he was still figuring out what direction he needed to take in his career, he would be steering the ship and she would be steering him.

Once they were back in his apartment things were quiet. It was closing in on two in the morning. It had been a long day, so they fell into bed. He snuggled her close, and for once he slept through the night.

Once he was fully awake the next morning, he texted Heinrich for breakfast and snuggled into her. He ran his hands over the curve of her soft hips, the mound of her belly, then he traced his fingers over her arms. The heat emanating between them warmed him to his very core. He kissed her head and breathed in her scent. Coconuts. She still smelled like the shampoo from their shower last night.

They had talked until the wee hours of the morning, until the pauses between their conversations drew longer and they both had drifted off.

Watching her, it started to become clearer what he

needed to do. First, he desperately needed time off. He would wrap up a few things this week before the rescheduled concert. He would also spend this week getting to the bottom of what was going on with Jacinda and the label. This was his last commitment with the label, it might be time to move on. He knew he didn't want to give up his career, but he needed to be able to trust those around him. Trusting himself was the first step to that.

Lexi started to stir in his arms. She let out a sleepy whimper and rocked her glorious ass into his growing erection. She pulled his hand so it was cupping her breast and he took the hint. He started rocking into her, gliding his cock between her legs, but not inside of her yet. They lay there gently rocking into each other, slow searching hands and gentle kisses and tenderness. It was the opposite of their powerful sex last night, but just what he needed.

He pulled away and got a condom from his drawer and rolled it down his already slick erection. Then he was inside of her, gently rocking into the build and bringing each other to climax in such a tender way he had to bite back tears. He loved her. It had only been a week and he knew that deep down.

That morning they hung out in bed, ate breakfast, and enjoyed each other. Neither one of them ready to deal with the car that would be coming in a few short hours to take her away.

But finally, that time had come. Lexi was packing her bag. He would give anything for her to stay longer. He was on his bed strumming his guitar as she shoved her phone charger in her bag.

"Well, I think that's everything," she said with a faraway smile.

"So, what's next?" he asked, setting down the guitar and sliding to the edge of the bed.

"Well, I have to work tomorrow. As much as I don't want to go back, I can't really afford more time off."

"You don't want to go back?" he asked. He was a little surprised by this, she seemed to really enjoy her job.

"Not really, I'd love some more time off. I've been working without a vacation since I was fifteen. That's over half my life."

"I thought you liked your job?"

"I guess I do. It beats cleaning rooms. I worked hard to get where I am. It's the best job I've ever had, but it doesn't mean I wouldn't love a life where I didn't have to work so hard all the time. But I mean that's life, what choice is there? Find a job that isn't too soul crushing and keep it."

The wheels in his head were turning, this could potentially change everything.

"What would you do with your time off?"

"I don't know. I've never given it much thought," she said with a shrug. "I would sleep, that much I know. I would do nothing. Then when I was all done doing nothing, which could potentially take a really long time, maybe I would travel. There are so many places I would love to see that I just haven't had the chance. Seeing that board from my closet reminded me of all the things I dreamed of doing, all the places I dreamed of going."

"I think that sounds fucking amazing. I've done my fair share of traveling, more than my fair share honestly, but there's still so many experiences I haven't had. I've seen the stage and the inside of lots of hotel rooms, but that's not seeing the world."

His phone buzzed on the table next to him. He knew what it said, and he didn't want to look at it, but he did.

"Looks like your car is here."

"Okay," she sighed, picking up her bags. "Let's do this."

It took every ounce of restraint he had not to cancel the car, and tell her to stay and quit her job, but he needed time to plan. She needed time to think and be sure. This sucked. He took the bag from her, and they made their way to the elevator. Once in the parking garage the driver got her bag. Liam wrapped his arms around her, holding her close to him, wishing they weren't about to be apart. He reminded himself that he had to fix his mess and that he would see her in a week. That felt like a long time right now.

He pulled back from her enough to kiss her slowly and with such tenderness. Breaking the kiss, he leaned his forehead against hers, tears burning in his sinuses. The words he wanted to say were at the tip of his tongue, but he swallowed them down. He cupped her face and kissed her one last time.

"This has been the best week of my life," she said with such honesty it broke him.

"I'll see you at the show next weekend."

She nodded, tears in her eyes.

"And I'm going to text you so much everyday you'll beg me to stop."

"Not a chance."

"And I'm going to facetime you every night."

"Even better."

He sighed and pressed another kiss to her trembling mouth. He pulled away, needing to rip off the band aid or he would whisk her right back up into bed and pretend all the stuff he had to deal with didn't exist. If he was going to make this work, he needed to give it a sturdy base to build the relationship on.

With all his will power he walked her over to the car and said goodbye. The car started its way out of the parking deck and Liam pulled out his phone.

Liam- I miss you already.

Lexi- Right back atcha.

Chapter 24

Lexi

The car ride home had been a long tearful one for Lexi, which wasn't like her. She usually had this no nonsense, sarcastic shell of protection around her. Liam had blown that all the way up. She wasn't sure how to proceed. When she let him in on the bench overlooking the falls, she thought it was safe because he was leaving. He was leaving and she would never see him again, so sharing the deep secrets she kept seemed safe. Why would a big star like Liam James care about the trials of her life? But she wasn't prepared for what happened afterward.

She was not prepared to fall in love with him and she certainly was not expecting for him to love her back. And while neither of them had said the words, she knew what she felt, and thought he just might feel the same way.

There were still a lot of logistics to work out. This whole thing could still blow up in her face, but she knew he was worth it. Yet here she was back in her sad little house, eating a disgusting frozen dinner.

Getting up, she tossed the whole thing in the trash and ordered a pizza. It was time she got out of the autopilot she had been trapped in. She was no longer in the survival mode that had almost killed her. She had a good job. She had this house. She had money in her savings. She had a brother who loved her, and just maybe, if she let them in, she could have a group of friends. That cookout had been nice, and the Smith's had started inviting her to all the holidays. She had declined their invitations because she just thought they were being nice. Maybe they were just being nice, but what's wrong with that? Just being nice can turn into real, lasting relationships.

The dream board was still on her table, taunting her. She wished things had worked out differently for the little girl who had made that board. She wished she had been able to follow her dreams, explore the world, and find out who she was. Liam would gladly help her fulfill her dreams. She knew that without a second thought. But the thing was, she didn't know what she wanted. She had never explored that because what would've the point? Her life was set for her the day her mom died. She hadn't made a choice since that day. Now that there were choices available to her, she was at a loss about what to do.

After switching over the laundry, there was a knock at the door. She got the pizza and settled on the couch, turning on a show she had seen a million times. Tomorrow she would go back to work and pretend like her life hadn't just been turned upside down.

Her phone vibrated on the table. She smiled when she saw who it was.

Liam- how do you feel about dick pics?

Lexi- In general not great, but for specific dick I'm all for it.

Liam- You better mean mine.

Lexi- *kissy face emoji*

Liam- photo uploading...

And there it was. His hard dick in his hand and all the sudden she couldn't remember why it was important to be back here. The ache between her legs certainly wasn't helping to remind her.

Her phone vibrated again with a facetime alert. She answered it and there was a naked Liam, lounging on his bed.

"My don't you look comfortable," she said.

"Wanna get comfortable with me?" He asked, with a cocked eyebrow.

"I do. I really do."

"Good. Why don't you go to bed and get a little more comfortable."

"I've never done anything like this. Are you sure I don't need an NDA for that."

"Get your fine ass in bed," he said with hungry eyes.

Liam

Liam woke up the next morning hard and wanting, which was no surprise to him after last night. Saturday night he would be performing his last concert of this tour. Lexi would be there in the audience, and he was going straight from that tour to a well-earned break. He didn't know exactly what that would look like, but he knew he wanted to be in Mystic Falls with Lexi. They would figure things out together. He thought about building a house in Mystic Falls with a recording studio.

He was also surprised he'd sent her a dick pic last night. His team definitely wouldn't be happy about that, but he trusted Lexi way more than he trusted his team these days. But that would be changing soon.

He got up and went into his kitchen and made himself a cup of tea and some eggs, then he texted Jacinda. It was time.

There was a knock at the door. He opened it to find Jacinda with a confused look on her face.

"There is something wrong with your door. The code didn't work. You should have Heinrich call someone to look at it," she said as she walked past him into the living room.

"Jacinda, we need to talk," he said. He knew he needed to fire her, but he wasn't looking forward to it.

She pulled out her phone. "Everything is set up for the rescheduled concert, but we do need to figure a time for you to meet with the label."

"I've been talking to Sue. She was looking over my contract last night, and it would seem that my contract ends with this tour."

She looked up at him, her eyes narrowed. "I'd have to check on that."

Liam knew damn well she knew and was just hoping that he didn't know. But Sue and an attorney she knew had been going over it, and this could all be over this weekend.

"I'm positive I'm right. I'll be taking a break after this tour and making some changes."

"What kind of changes?" She asked, her eyes still uncertain.

"For starters, I'm going to be taking the driver's seat of my own career. After the scandal I stepped back, and I don't like the direction things have taken."

"What exactly are you referring to?"

"I am referring to that ridiculous list of yours and also the NDA's."

"That is all just part of life on the road, Liam. It protects you and the label."

"I don't give a fuck about the label. And I just need to say this. After the concert on Saturday, I think we're done too."

"Are you firing me?" She asked.

"Yes, I am. You did so much shit behind my back. You took advantage of me and the bad place I was in. I think it is best we part ways after the concert while I try and figure out where I go from here."

"Liam, you can't fire me," she spat back at him.

"I most certainly can."

"No. You can't. I don't work for you," she said plainly.

"I'm sorry, what?" he asked.

"I am an employee of the label. My father hired me to make sure you didn't fuck up your image any more than you already have. Sure, the gender nonconformity stuff works for you, but your image couldn't handle another scandal."

"My gender expression and sexuality are not a scandal. They are part of who I am, a part of the music I make. I am a success because of those things not despite them. Jesus, Jacinda. Do you have any idea what my fans love about me?"

"Yes! We've polled them. They love the fantasy of you. That is what you give them night after night."

That thought threatened to spin him out. He felt the walls closing in. Was that really all he was? A fantasy? A pretty face with a nice voice? Closing his eyes, he took a deep breath.

There were letters, hundreds of them covering his wall in his music room, all telling him differently. Those letters told him that his music and self-expression gave them the courage to be who they truly were. Those letters told him that they were able to find a safe space in his fan community. The crying faces in his concert when he sang his songs about finding your own way and your own family, told him that he was more than a pretty face. He was more than a fantasy. Sure, there was an element of fantasy to him, but he had to believe there was more. And if what she said was true then the sacrifice wasn't worth it, but he knew he was more.

"Jacinda. I need you to leave. I'm parting ways with you and the label after the concert. It's clear the people profiting off of my music, off my very soul, don't have my best interest at heart anymore."

Jacinda stood and walked out. He let out a big sigh, and walked into his music room, eyes on the massive wall and all the letters. Then he sat at his piano and started writing a song. It was the first song he had written since London. It was a love song. A love song to his fans and to Lexi. She had reminded him why he did this. Reminded him that he didn't need to sacrifice every piece of himself. There were some pieces just for him.

But more importantly, there were some parts that he would allow her to see and keep safe. He trusted her to do that. She would be his safe harbor, and he would be the wind in her sail. They both needed something different from each other, but they fit perfectly.

If he wasn't certain before, he was certain now. He was

in love with Lexi Turner, and they would find a way, because she was the way.

Taking a deep breath, he sat down at the piano and it all just came pouring out of him.

Her song.

Chapter 25

Liam

Liam was making plans for the future. It was a much different future than he had imagined two weeks ago. The timing was amazing. If he hadn't met Lexi when he did, he would have signed on for another album. The label would have him off recording somewhere and he would still be lost. But he had found her, and he learned the truth about the people around him. He was excited for what the future would bring for the first time in a long time.

He had called his original manager last night and discussed the direction he wanted to take things after bringing her back on board. She had stepped aside so people could come to deal with his PR and he had let them, but it was time to bring back the people he trusted.

Looking out the giant window, Liam sat in a boardroom waiting to meet with his record label and lawyers. With him was his original manager and a lawyer she trusted who he planned to hire. All of them were waiting for the execs, who were apparently trying to prove a point by making them wait. As far as Liam was concerned, he had all the time in the world. If this was all going to be over soon, he would sit in this room all day.

After twenty minutes, the doors pushed open, and in rushed six men in suits and Jacinda, who sat next to her father looking smug.

"It's nice to see you Liam." Jacinda's father said. "We've been trying to schedule this meeting for days. I'm glad you have finally decided to meet with us. Who do you have with you?"

"Well, as I'm sure Jacinda told you, I am making some changes after the tour. I'm bringing back Sue and she has recommended Mr. Thomas here to be my new lawyer."

The man sitting next to him put the papers in the folder and closed it, reaching his hand out. "I'm Mr. Thomas."

"Mr. Moore," Jacinda's father shook it without even looking at him.

"Well, we can certainly welcome them to the team, but I wouldn't recommend any further changes to the team at this time. After your show tomorrow, we have some spaces available to you for your next album. We reserved a spot for you in Paris, Prague, and if you're feeling homey, one in the Colorado Mountains. All these homes come equipped with a recording studio. We have Miles Flynn ready to produce your new album." He slid over some paperwork to Liam. He looked at it just out of curiosity. All these places were incredible and would be a dream to record in, but they weren't his dream.

"I'm afraid I'm not interested in any of these. Mr. Thomas reviewed my contract and after my concert tomorrow I have no further contractual obligations."

The man's eye twitched. "I would have to check on that, but we've been working well for years."

"We have, but it was recently brought to my attention

just how much was going on behind the scenes without my knowledge. Because of that I have decided to make some changes," Liam said calmly.

"I see," he said coldly. "What changes are you hoping to make?"

"After the concert I am done working with this team and this label. I'll be taking some time off before my next album to regroup. From there Sue and Mr. Thomas will help me with the next steps."

"I'm not sure that is a wise decision."

"And why is that?"

"I'm not sure if you saw the headlines this morning, but it seems you find yourself in the midst of yet another scandal Mr. James," he said as the corner of his mouth twitched, holding back a sneer.

"Another scandal? What are you talking about?"

"Jacinda?" He gestured to his daughter.

Jacinda smiled at him and slid a piece of paper across the table to him. His heart dropped as he saw it. There before him was a fuzzy picture of him and Lexi kissing after his concert while they waited for the car. This was a protected area. The only people allowed there were the workers. This shouldn't have happened. Picking it up to inspect it further the headline, the fucking headline, filled him with more rage than he knew how to handle. That was fucked up. Not only was it insulting to him and the relationship between him and Lexi, but it was unnecessarily hurtful toward her. He needed to make sure she was okay, but he didn't seem to have his phone on him. Fuck!

"Do you think your little team is equipped to handle this kind of scandal? Isn't this why you brought us on?"

"Well, a fucking lot of good it did, with bullshit like this," he said as he slid the paper back at them. They could fucking choke on it for all he cared.

"It is my understanding that you recently changed the rules Ms. Moore put in place to help scandals like this from popping up. You are the cause of this scandal and all the pain it will bring to this poor woman. You should read the article, there are some really hurtful things said about her. Not only is it bad for your image, but now another innocent person has been brought into the mess all over again."

Well, that did it. That shut him up. All his righteous fury gone in an instant. He was right. He didn't need to read the article to know the things it would have to say about someone like Lexi. This was exactly why he was against a relationship in the beginning, he knew she would get hurt like this. He had dealt with that for years, but Lexi... She didn't deserve the hurt this would cause. She had helped him find his way through the storm, and this is how he would repay her, by bringing scrutiny and cruelty to her doorstep. That thought made him sick to his stomach.

A warm hand found his on the table. A warm hand in this room of opportunistic vultures that care nothing about him and only had fake concern for the woman he loved. The woman he hoped loved him even though this was going to cause her so much pain. Looking over at Sue, she offered a warm smile. She had stepped aside last time when Liam thought this was a good decision, but this time she wasn't stepping aside.

"Be that as it may," Liam said, trying to sound strong through his wavering voice. "My decision stands. After tomorrow my last contractual obligation is complete, we're done. You can talk it out with my manager and legal counsel, but I'm done here."

He stood and walked out. He needed to talk to Lexi.

Where the fuck was his phone? Above the large reception desk, he checked the time, five thirty on a Friday. They were sure playing games keeping him there this long. He was done with their games, Sue and Mr. Thomas could deal with them.

Hopefully his car was still there. Checking outside he didn't see it, but he did hear some people whispering behind him. He would give anything to be a normal person right now and just hail a taxi and get home. Instead, he went back inside and waited for his team to finish up whatever they were talking about without him. As soon as they were done, he would go home and call Lexi. He would make sure she was okay and then they could start their life together.

One more night, one more show, and then they would figure it out together. At least that's what he hoped. He sat down on the couch waiting for his team, trying to silence the voice that told him he wasn't worth the hassle.

Finally, around six thirty, his manager and new lawyer came out of the room.

"I was wondering how far you would get without this," she said as she gave him his phone.

He took a quick peek at it, nothing from Lexi. Maybe she didn't know yet. She wasn't online much, and she never even fully googled him in the beginning, so maybe she wasn't aware yet. But he knew whether she was unaware or not, there were hundreds of tabloid journalists and bloggers working their magic to try and find out the identity of the mystery woman he was kissing. That thought of strangers casting judgment on her for her body made him see red. Closing his eyes, he momentarily pushed away the rage to focus on the current problem at hand.

"Sorry I stormed out like that, but I really needed to get away. What's the word?"

"You're done with them after tomorrow night. You have no contractual obligation to continue with this label. There will be some legal issues with some of the songs. They still own the tracks you performed that were written by other musicians, but you were smart and protected your own music. You leave with all the rights to those songs. We can figure out what that looks like when you're ready. I know you are wanting a break."

Honestly, that was better than he had hoped. He knew that they didn't have a legal leg to stand on, but that doesn't always stop major corporations. But it was almost over. He would perform tomorrow, then he was free. But right now, he needed to get home and check on Lexi.

Chapter 26

Lexi

It was Friday night and Lexi was getting ready for the concert tomorrow. Her floor was covered in clothes because she only had a few outfits suitable for a concert and Liam had already seen her in most of them. Over in Glendale there was a store that sold clothes in her size, but none that she really liked. She was almost strictly an online shopper these days. Being short and plus size meant finding her size was tricky.

The thought of letting Liam know she was struggling with this did cross her mind. She knew he would work some magic and somehow have new clothes delivered on her step by magic forest creatures, but she didn't want to take advantage of him. Using his connections like that just felt wrong but being with someone who was known for their style while not really having one herself didn't feel great. But time and money and of course her body had made being interested in fashion not really available to her, but that might be changing now.

In the end, she settled on the outfit she wore for their first date but with some boots she hadn't had many opportunities to wear. She wasn't even sure why she had ever bought something as impractical as tall black leather boots with a high rainbow heel. She could definitely wear them at a Liam James concert. Self-expression was the biggest star at his concert. She loved that. She was so excited to see him perform again, and maybe have some after concert fun that would make her blush for weeks. She had only officially been with him for a week, but it felt like part of her was missing when they were apart. It was a new feeling, but a welcome one all the same.

And he had been so attentive while they were apart. Good morning texts, random texts throughout the day, sweet ones and not so sweet ones. And they had video chatted every night. A couple of those nights had been sexy, which was very new to her, but also something she enjoyed. But all that being said, she couldn't wait to see him tomorrow and be close to him. They both came close to saying I love you this week, but not yet. It was coming though; she could feel it.

Just as she was finishing packing her bag her phone buzzed on her dresser. She smiled, hoping it was Liam, but it was Poppy.

Poppy- Hey Lexi, have you been online much today?

Lexi- Not really why?

Poppy- I'm coming over.

Lexi- Why?

Lexi- What's going on?

Lexi- Poppy, you're kind of freaking me out.

The absence of her response told her all she needed to know. Poppy was on her way, but why? There could only be one reason, and she was fairly certain she knew what it was.

She pulled up google and once again typed in Liam James. She scrolled down, most of the major hits were the same, but then she saw something new. A headline that hadn't been there before. She clicked on the story and there was a picture of him leaning against the wall holding her to him as he kissed her after the concert. That headline. Fuck. She knew this was part of it, but right now that wasn't much of a comfort.

Sitting down on her bed, her heart started to race and breathing increased. She never had a panic attack before, but she'd seen Josh have them, and this was definitely how they looked. Closing her eyes, she took some deep breaths and then counted down her senses: five things she could see, four things she could feel, three things she could hear, two things she could smell, and one thing she could taste. That was something one of the therapists she had taken Josh to had taught them. It helped to ground her in her body.

The sound of her front door flying open didn't even startle her.

"Lexi, where are you?" Poppy called.

"I'm upstairs."

Before she knew it Poppy was standing at her bedroom door with a concerned look on her face. "You didn't wait to check it out before I came over, did you?"

Lexi shook her head. She was still processing.

"You know that article is bullshit, right?"

Lexi bit her lip and nodded. She did know the article

was bullshit. She knew what existed between her and Liam was real and not some weird fetish. She didn't care what strangers said about her body, that was their problem. The part that scared her that it was also Liam's problem. This was exactly why he had not wanted to start anything serious with her. He didn't want a scandal, but here it was anyway.

"Are you okay?" Poppy asked, concern coloring her voice.

"Yeah, I'm okay, I mean the internet is a trash place, especially if you're fat. I get it, it sucks, but it is what it is."

Poppy nodded and waited for her to continue. And while Lexi had hoped to leave it at that, Poppy wasn't really one to let things go. But this was one of those moments, like the moment at the waterfall with Liam where she chose to be brave. She could keep it all in and push people away, or she could let people in. And Poppy was family. It was time Lexi started letting go of the past and breaking down the walls she built around herself.

So, she took a deep breath and continued, "Clearly there is something going on with me and Liam. I'm not one hundred percent sure what that is, we have only known each other for two weeks, but it feels pretty fucking special." Pausing to take a breath, she was surprised at the shakiness, but she pushed back her tears and continued. "At first he told me it was just the weekend because he couldn't have another scandal." She took another shaky breath as a tear rolled down her cheek. "We thought we were careful, but here we are. Now I'm scared he is going to change his mind."

That was it. Saying it out loud wrecked her. She crumbled on her bed, her head in her hands unable to hold back the tears. Poppy was right there, pulling Lexi into a hug. She held her close as Lexi cried on her shoulder. Trusting people to see her pain wasn't easy, but she knew she could trust Poppy. And as scary as that was, it did feel good to have someone there with her.

She brushed her hair as Lexi cried. "Shhh, It's okay. I could see what was going on between you guys. It's something special. I'm sure he won't change his mind. Have you talked to him today?"

Lexi lifted her head and wiped her eyes. "No, he said he was going to be busy today in meetings, so I probably wouldn't talk to him until tonight." Glancing over at her clock, it was almost eight and she still hadn't heard anything. That wasn't like him.

"I'm sure he'll call. Are you okay though? I don't know how much of the article you read, but I know what it's like existing in this world in a fat body and how shitty people can be."

"Yeah, I learned to have a tough skin about that a long time ago. People's opinions of me are their problem. I don't like what those people said about me but fuck them. I just worry about Liam..." She stopped there, feeling the tears coming again.

Poppy reached out and put her hand on her knee. "Okay, if that's the case you're going to call Liam right now and check in with him. I'm sure he's just as pissed as you are, but I'm also certain he is not changing his mind. Why don't you call him? Where is your phone?" She asked with her eyes scanning the room. "What's going on? Why is your entire wardrobe scattered on the floor?"

Lexi surveyed the room and chuckled to herself. Her previous dilemma of nothing to wear now seemed silly. "I'm going to Liam's concert tomorrow, but I have nothing to wear. My two best outfits I wore on our first date and the first concert I saw. I had just decided to re-wear the first outfit, but now if there is going to be scrutiny maybe I shouldn't... maybe I shouldn't even go."

"Nope! You're going. And don't worry, between me and Hannah, I'm sure we can get you something amazing to wear." Poppy picked up her phone and started texting.

"You don't have to do that."

Poppy put her phone down and looked at Lexi. Just looked at her.

"I'm serious. I'm sure what I have will be fine."

"Lexi. I will find you something amazing to wear. Of course, wear those boots, those are some killer 'fuck me' boots, but don't worry about this. Having friends with similar body types isn't a perk fat people often get, so just enjoy it. Now you call Liam, and I'm sure he'll tell you everything is fine."

Unearthing her phone from the piles on her bed, Poppy tossed it to Lexi. "I'll be over first thing with an outfit for the concert." She pulled her into a hug

Just like that she was gone as quickly as she came. She had said it last year and she would say it again, she was a force of nature. It was best to just go with her. And right now, Lexi was more than happy to be in the Poppy storm. The Liam one was a bit scarier.

She closed her eyes, trying to find the courage to call him, but just at that moment her phone started buzzing in her hand. The screen read incoming call Liam.

"Hello," she answered weakly.

"Are you okay?" he said quickly.

"I'm fine--"

"I'm so fucking sorry, Lexi. I was scared of this. I'm not sure why I thought we could do it differently, I should've known. Did you read it?"

"Just the headline, I figured I should stop there."

"That's probably a good call. It was all shit. All of it. Are you sure you're okay?"

"I'm fine, are you okay?"

"I'm pissed. I want to find whoever leaked that picture and fire them. I want to sue the tabloids for harassment. I want to plead with all the people engaging with this trash online to stop and realize we are all fucking people not just fodder for their amusement."

She'd never heard him like this before. He was so angry, and he had every right to be. Lexi wasn't ready for this to be over, but it was his career and they had only known each other for two weeks. The connection had been amazing, but he'd been building something incredible for years. He said they could try for something else, but they had tried and what he was worried about had happened. Lexi didn't feel panic setting in, she felt her walls going up... and that was much worse.

"I'm sorry this all happened Liam. I know this is what you were afraid of, and here we are. You said only a week, so if that's all we have, that's okay. I will remember it fondly."

"It's not fucking okay, Lexi. Is this it for you? Are you done?" The pleading in his voice shocked her. "I wasn't afraid of a fucking scandal. I was afraid of another person walking away from me because my life is too much. I get it if that's what you're doing, but please, give me a chance to fix this. I don't know how, but please don't walk away. Things are about to change for me in some pretty major ways. I can include you in that, we can figure out how this best works for us --"

"Liam, stop." The sound of his sniffle just about broke her heart. "I don't want it to be the end. I just thought you might because of everything. I don't care what people say about me. I only knew because Poppy texted to check up on me. I can easily stay offline until this all blows over. I just don't want to be a burden on your career."

"Oh, thank god, Lexi. I can have a career and be with you. I made some big changes today and I still have another meeting tonight to make sure everything is good, I just wanted to check on you."

The relief in his voice was palpable, and she felt her own relief too. They were okay, and that's all that mattered.

"We're good. If you have time, call me when you are done tonight, if not I'll see you tomorrow."

"I lo.... I can't wait to see you. I'll call you tonight if I can."

"Okay, don't worry about this though. I'm fine as long as you're fine."

"If I could kiss you right now I would, gorgeous."

"Right back atcha."

She hung up the phone and tossed it on her bed. Breathing a sigh of relief, she flopped onto her bed and the mountain of clothes. Tomorrow she would be seeing Liam in apparently borrowed clothes from her new friends. Her Lean Cuisine life had definitely made some changes in the past two weeks, and she was thrilled. She got up and started putting away her clothes, excited for what tomorrow held.

Chapter 27

Liam

After he got off the phone with Lexi, the relief he felt was palpable. Knowing she wasn't going anywhere, even in the midst of a scandal, was the reassurance he needed.

After rummaging around in the fridge for food, Heinrich entered the kitchen.

"Mr. James, Mr. Diaz is here to see you."

"Perfect, bring him in."

Liam headed to the living room. Fame came with many perks and getting late appointments with a realtor was one of them.

Heinrich showed Mr. Diaz into the living room. He had on a nice crisp suit and his sleek black hair was flawless.

He reached out and shook Liam's hand. "Hello Mr. James, I am happy to make your acquaintance. I hear you are looking to buy some property in Mystic Falls, is that correct?"

"Yeah, what do you have for me?" He asked as they sat on the couch.

"There are a couple properties that might interest you.

One is an old farmhouse; the property butts up against an orchard and we should move on that one quickly if you want it. It comes with a big old barn. It would need lots of renovation, but I think it could meet your needs. The other is a five-acre lot. It is right next to the state park that has the falls. Both options are reasonably priced. You could build on the property or renovate the old farmhouse."

He sat out two folders on the coffee table before Liam. He picked up one and opened it. Pictures of a cute farmhouse and a big red barn, it was beautiful and picturesque.

"I thought you might be able to convert the barn into a studio. The structure is in good condition. I could help you find a team to work on it, if you choose to go that route."

Liam nodded and continued flipping through the paper. He set it down then picked up the other. Inside that one was pictures of land, and he could see how close it was to the falls.

"That one will clearly take more time, but it will be easy to get everything ready for water and power. Sometimes that can be an issue building a new structure, but this one is pretty straightforward."

"These look amazing. I'll talk to some people and get back to you. I'm hoping to get started on this soon."

Both of the men rose, and Liam reached out and shook his hand. "Heinrich will show you out. I appreciate you meeting me this late. My schedule can be a little crazy sometimes."

"It was my pleasure, Mr. James. I look forward to working with you." He turned and followed Heinrich out of the apartment.

Liam walked over and gazed out the window. It was twilight and the city was falling into that magic time of night. He craved Lexi next to him. He wanted to snake his arms around her waist and snuggle in close, smelling her coconut shampoo. He wanted to hear her dry, sarcastic wit. And, if he was being honest, he also wanted her in his bed, his face buried between her legs. But there would be time for that. Tomorrow actually.

He went to his room and video called her. It was time for their nightly talks, and he was anxious to see her face tonight. He was really hoping she wasn't hurting. She was beautiful to him. He hoped she felt that way, but he was willing to spend the rest of his life making sure she did. It would be his new life's work. Now that things were back on track, he wanted her by his side. Here's hoping she wanted the same thing.

Chapter 28

Lexi

Earlier in the week Liam had tried to talk Lexi into taking a car, but she was perfectly capable of driving. The town was only two hours away. So, Lexi got herself ready in the amazing outfit that Poppy brought over that morning and headed to the concert. She was beginning to regret her decision when she went to pick up the ticket Liam had left her. She could feel the eyes following her. The whispers wondering if she was the mystery girl. She would much rather be backstage with Liam than dealing with this.

Lexi sighed with relief as she made her way to the VIP seating. There were many of the perks to dating the rock star, and this was one of her favorites. She hated crowds and often felt claustrophobic in them. This allowed her to be a part of this whole experience and have her own space. Which she was especially grateful for with people recognizing her. Of course, she wasn't ashamed, but she did not like the extra attention. She wasn't sure of the best way to deal with it. Liam was a pro at this, quite literally. There were a few other reserved chairs in the area, but right now it was just her and she was more than happy with that.

She pulled out her phone and texted Liam good luck and slid it back into her purse.

As the opening acts started, she was joined in the box by a couple men in suits and a familiar face, one she wasn't really happy to see. Jacinda. Lexi knew Liam was thinking about firing her, but it clearly hadn't happened yet. Maybe they had come to an understanding? That was his business. She could be polite to just about anyone. Working in the service industry gave her an easy demeanor of steel.

"Oh hello, Lexi, is it? I'm sorry, it's so hard to keep track." she asked with a fake smile.

"That's correct. How are you doing, Jacinda?" Lexi said, biting her tongue.

"I'm fine, just getting things set up for Liam's next album."

Lexi just nodded. Liam had already told her that he was taking a break. This woman was something else.

"I'm so sorry about the picture that got leaked. They said some truly awful things," Jacinda said with mock sympathy.

"I didn't read it, and I don't really care what people have to say about me. I'm comfortable in my own skin and other people's opinions of me are really none of my business."

"Wow... that's so brave of you. I wish I was as confident as you are."

Lexi looked to the stage as the opening act was starting, glad this meant her conversation with Jacinda was over. It's funny how being told that she was brave and confident could feel like such a backhanded compliment. But it would seem Jacinda wasn't quite done talking.

"I'm glad you can ignore it. Sadly, we don't have that luxury," she said loudly over the music.

"What do you mean?"

"It's just that Liam's image is such a big part of his career. We're trying to decide the best way to handle it. So much of him is the fantasy. And if he's dating anyone it can be an issue. Let alone someone like you?"

Lexi's blood was starting to boil. She was being as nice as she could, but this woman was ridiculous.

"Someone like me?" Lexi asked, her smile finally starting to falter.

"Yeah, someone his fans wouldn't... expect him to be with, you know what I mean,"

"No, I don't."

"If I may speak candidly," she said.

Speak candidly? Lexi was almost afraid of what that would look like if she wasn't already speaking candidly.

"I'm not sure what is going on between you and Liam, he does this all the time. But I would just ask yourself if it is worth it. All these people love Liam. He means so much to them. His music and who he is helps people be who they truly are. He's important and I would hate to see that damaged with another scandal."

Lexi just looked at her as the air huffed out of her lungs. She wasn't sure what to say.

"Well, if Liam is so important to his fans, then wouldn't they want him to be authentically himself," she asked.

"And you think you know what that is? You have known him for two weeks. Right now, he's a man in desperate need of a little time off who's making decisions based on that. I've been with him for years. Trust me, I know who he is, and his fans do too."

Lexi didn't know how to respond to that. Could she really claim to know him better? As much as it pained her to admit Jacinda was right, she might be. She had only known him for two weeks. That's not enough time to really know anyone, no matter how connected her and Liam seemed to be.

She turned her back on Jacinda and walked a few steps away and enjoyed the rest of the opening act. She couldn't wait to see Liam again, both on stage and off.

As the opening was clearing off and the crowd was getting ready for Liam, she pulled out her phone to check what time it was. She had four missed calls from Josh and a handful of texts. She opened them and her heart stopped.

> Josh - Poppy and I were in a car accident. I am ok, but Poppy is in the hospital.

> Josh - I'm sorry to bother you, but I just needed to talk to you.

Then a couple other texts with the hospital information for Poppy. Her heart was in her throat. She needed to get to Josh. Like right now. She turned to leave.

"Jacinda, I need to leave. My brother and his wife were in a car accident. Please tell Liam why I left and that I'm very sorry, but I have to go."

"Of course, I will, oh you poor thing. Go be with your family. Family is the most important thing."

Lexi nodded and made her way out of the box. She made her way through the whispering crowd of people who were trying to figure out if she was the woman from the photo, but she didn't care about them right now. All she could think about was Josh. This would be scary for anyone, but she knew Josh had to be freaking out. Losing their mother at a young age to a car accident left its fair share of trauma on both of them and having his wife in the hospital because of an accident must have him in a bad headspace.

As soon as she was out of the arena and on her way to her car, she pulled out her phone to call Josh. It went to voicemail.

"I'm on my way, Josh. I should be there in about an hour." They were in Glendale, so that was a little closer than having to go all the way to Mystic Falls. She texted him for good measure that she was on her way.

She got in her car and left Liam a message as well. Then she pulled out and made her way to the hospital.

Lexi made it to the hospital in record time. The concert would still be going on, but she needed to find them and make sure they were both alright. She walked right up to the nurse's station.

"Hi, I'm looking for Poppy Turner."

She got the room number, and she was off through the maze of the ER to find Josh. She got to room 408b and knocked quietly. Josh answered the door with a panicked look on his face. She had grown accustomed to it over the years, but it still broke her heart. She also noticed that in addition to his expression, was a bump on his head and a tiny butterfly bandage over a small cut.

"You're hurt," she said as she reached up to his head.

"I'm okay. I'm so glad you came," he said, wrapping his arms around her. "I didn't know if you would."

"Of course, I came. I came as soon as I got the message."

"I'm sorry to pull you away from the concert. I just didn't know what else to do. Poppy's family is here. They went to the cafeteria while they took Poppy to run some tests. They didn't want to leave me, but I just needed a second to breathe. I need to be here if they come back with any news." He collapsed in the chair, his head in his hands.

Lexi sat next to him and rubbed his back.

"How is she? How are you?"

"They think she's going to be ok, but she broke her arm and is banged up pretty bad. I'm fine, I got this," he said pointing to the small gash on his forehead with stitches, "but no concussion."

"Josh, how could you even for a second doubt I'd be here?"

"I don't know, things have just been off between us lately. I'm not sure what you're going through, but I miss you."

"Oh Josh, I miss you too. I think I was just trying to give you space, but also maybe trying to protect myself and ignore how lonely I felt. But I'm done doing that. We're good. I promise."

"That makes me feel better because I have something else to tell you. There is a reason they're being extra careful with Poppy. This isn't the way we wanted to tell everyone, but she's pregnant."

"Oh my god, Josh! That's amazing! Congratulations!"

"Thanks. We were waiting to tell everyone just a little bit longer, but then this happened. I'm so scared something is wrong, but she keeps trying to reassure me everything is fine. They are running some tests right now to make sure the baby is okay."

"I'm sure the baby is going to be just fine. What happened?"

"We were on the way home from Glendale when the car in front of us slammed on its brakes to avoid hitting a deer and I swerved to avoid them, but then we went in the ditch and the car rolled."

Lexi just hugged him close. They were always quite a pair when they hugged because Josh had a well over a foot on her, but they fit together. They had only each other for so long, they knew how to be there for each other.

The door opened and in walked the whole Smith crew. Gran handed Josh a sandwich and a bottle of water. Jackson sat in the chair next to him.

"So, I snuck a peek at Poppy's chart, and things are looking good. The baby's heartbeat is fine, and Poppy is okay. The worst part of the whole thing is going to be that she can't have the good pain killers for the broken arm. I think they are setting it right now." Josh pulled Jackson into a big hug and Jackson patted him on the back. "It's good to have a man on the inside," Jackson said as he pulled away.

"Thank you. Thank all of you so much for being here, it means a lot," Josh choked out.

"Of course, dear, that's what family is for," Gran said with a pat to his leg.

"So, you got pulled away from the Liam James concert?" Sam asked Lexi.

"Yeah, but of course I came as soon as I got the message. I'm just glad everyone is okay."

They all visited until Poppy came back. Lexi took a peek at her phone to check the time and see if Liam had texted her. It was after eleven so the concert should be over, but still no word. They decided to keep Poppy overnight for observation. The Smith family left, leaving Poppy and Josh to try and get some sleep.

"Do you want me to go pick up anything for you guys?" Lexi asked Josh.

"Actually, that would be great. Thank you."

"No problem." It was the least she could do. Josh texted her a list of things and told her where to find them. She set off to Mystic Falls. It would be about an hour round trip. She could handle that.

Once she got in her car, she looked at her phone, still nothing from Liam. She didn't like that, but there were more important things to deal with right now.

Chapter 29

Liam

Liam had just wrapped up his encore. Throughout the concert he kept looking at the box Lexi was supposed to be in, but he couldn't spot her. Maybe she got sat somewhere else? He wasn't sure but he couldn't wait to see her after the show, hopefully to have a repeat of the last show. He'd had some pretty amazing sexual encounters in his day, but that one had to be the best, and this time the end would be much better with him knowing he was done with the label.

He made his way to the dressing room to wait for Lexi. After he had been there awhile, the door opened he turned and rushed forward, only to be pulled up short when he saw it was Jacinda.

"Hello Jacinda, thanks for all your help tonight. It's been a pleasure working with you," he lied through his teeth. "Can you find Lexi for me? Then if you meet up with Sue, I'm sure you guys can finish up the night."

"I actually wanted to talk to you about Lexi," she walked towards him with a sympathetic look on her face.

"What's going on?" He asked suspiciously, his eyes narrowed on her.

"Lexi left."

"Left? What do you mean she left?"

"Before you even got on stage. Right after the opening act. I think the whole article was getting to her. People can be so cruel, you know."

"What the fuck happened?"

"I don't know. She just said to tell you sorry."

He collapsed on the couch. His head was spinning. This could not be happening again. His head dropped to his hands and his chest was tight. There had to be more to the story.

"Did she say anything else? She seemed okay last time I talked to her." He was replaying the conversations and all the texts and anything for a hint that something was wrong. He couldn't point to anything. Not a single damn thing. "Fuck!" He got up off the couch in a search for his phone. He needed to call her right now.

"I'm so sorry Liam, but at least we know this now before it went on too long. Better it be now when there weren't feelings involved yet."

He turned on her with an icy glare. "What the fuck, Jacinda? There are fucking feelings involved. I love her!"

Jacinda looked like she had been slapped in the face. "You don't love her; you've only known her for a couple weeks."

"Don't you dare tell me how I fucking feel. I love her and I know she loves me, and if she walked out, it is because something is wrong," he said while he was tearing apart the room. "Fuck! Where the fuck is my phone? I've got to call her now."

"Liam, let's just get you back to the city and we can figure out what is next."

He turned to her, his frantic energy turning to an icy one. "Jacinda, what aren't you telling me?"

"I don't know what you're talking about."

"Where is my phone?"

"Did you check your bag?"

"Yes, I fucking checked my bag." He was no longer panicking or frantic. He didn't know what had happened, but he knew Jacinda was behind it.

"I'll see what I can do."

"Jacinda, I need my phone and then I need you gone. I will have you escorted off the premises if I must."

"You're serious aren't you. You're going to have me escorted off the premises? After all I've done for you? I fucking saved your career. I made you Liam fucking James!" She was screaming at him. He had never seen her like this. She was coming undone. "I did everything my father said. I protected your image. I worked day and fucking night for you. And now you are going to throw all of it away for her," she spat at him with such disdain.

"What the fuck are you even talking about?"

"My father put me in charge of you after the scandal. I kept you safe."

"You kept me miserable and isolated."

"I kept you scandal free."

"But at what cost, Jacinda? Fuck, I am a person. I'm allowed to make my own decisions. I'm allowed to decide what my career is worth."

"I thought if you saw how easily the media would turn on her, that it would pull your head out of your ass, but apparently not."

"What?" The pieces of the puzzle all began to slot into

place. What the fuck had she done?

"You are just so intent on fucking it all up."

"It was you. You leaked the image of me and Lexi."

"Yes! But I did it for your own good. I thought if you saw the way the media treated her you might change your mind. You can't be with someone like her."

While she was talking Liam stood up and walked to the door. He was fuming. He knew she was desperate, but he didn't think she was capable of this. He opened the door and yelled "Security."

"Are you fucking serious right now, Liam?"

"I very much am. I would say it's been a pleasure, but I think we both know that would be a lie. And if I recall, when you started working as my manager you signed an NDA yourself did you not?"

Her eyes narrowed on his.

"Come on, I can't be the only one seeing the poetic justice there. I found out about this because of an NDA and now BECAUSE of an NDA I could sue your ass for releasing that photo." Two big men in black shirts showed up. "Please show Ms. Moore the door."

"You're done, Liam, if you keep fucking up like this. And here's your phone if you're so intent on ruining your own career from some random girl from bumfuck nowhere."

The men led her away as she threw the phone at Liam. He took a breath. He still didn't quite believe what had just happened. He was terrified of what she may have told Lexi. He knew she had overstepped all kinds of boundaries, but he didn't think she was capable of this. He had to make this right.

He picked up his phone that had fallen to the floor in all the commotion and looked at it for the first time since mic check.

There were a handful of texts from Lexi and a voicemail. He quickly decided to listen to her voicemail first, knowing he could tell more from the sound of her voice. He hit play and held the phone to his ear.

He was instantly hit with a wave of emotions. Relief, because thank fuck Jacinda hadn't fucked things up. Anger, because Jacinda was fucking lying to him again. But then most of all, concern. Her brother had been in an accident. He knew the dynamics of their relationship, and knew she had to be upset. And since that dynamic was created because of a tragic car accident, they were both probably pretty deep in their own trauma. He needed to get to her ASAP.

He checked the text messages and she had sent him the hospital she was at. He ordered a car right away and hopped in the shower while he waited.

The car was waiting for him when he finished. He called Lexi, but it went straight to voicemail. He texted her he was on his way and the car took off. Glendale was only a little over an hour away.

Finally, after what felt like an eternity, he was at the emergency room entrance. He wore a cardigan and hat, hoping to blend in as much as possible. The nurse's reception area was right in front.

"Hi, I'm here to see Poppy...." Oh no, he didn't know her last name. "Oh, and Josh Turner, they were in a car accident."

"Right." She started typing on her computer and looked back up at him. "They're just about to be admitted to the non-emergency part of the hospital, so I'm afraid you'll have to wait until tomorrow to see them."

"Thank you for your help." He turned to check his phone to see if Lexi had texted him, but then he saw her coming in carrying a bag. She looked up at him, eyes wide and her lips parted.

"What are you doing here?" She asked breathlessly.

He ran right over to her and wrapped her in his arms, and she clung to him. "Is everyone okay?" he asked softly in her ear as he stroked her back. She nodded against his cheek and let out a shuddering breath.

She pulled away and went to the reception desk. "Is Poppy Turner still in her room? I have an overnight bag for her and her husband."

"They haven't been moved yet, head on back."

Liam looked at the reception desk clerk, who just smiled softly and nodded. He was instantly at Lexi's side, taking the bag from her and holding her hand as she led the way through the hospital doors.

Knocking quietly, she entered the hospital room. Poppy was sleeping in the bed. She looked pretty banged up and her arm was in a cast. Josh stood to greet them at the door. He seemed fine, except for a small cut above his left eye that had been stitched up.

"That's gonna leave a pretty wicked scar," Liam said with a smile. "I'm sorry to intrude, but I'm glad you're all okay."

Josh smiled at him, "I'm glad you're here. I'm sorry I pulled Lexi away from your show."

"No worries. There'll be other concerts."

"How is she?" Lexi asked as she snaked her arm around Liam's waist.

"Good, she's sleeping now, clearly," he said quietly. "We should be out of here tomorrow."

"Do you want me to stay with you?" Lexi asked, her concern for her brother written squarely on her face.

"No, I'm fine--"

"Josh, I'm serious, say the word and I'll stay." She meant it too. Liam knew that, even if it meant sitting out in the waiting room all night, she would.

"I'm okay. You guys should head home."

"If you're sure..."

"I'm sure." He pulled Lexi into a big hug. "Thank you for this," he said, holding up the bag.

"Of course, do you need anything else before I go?" There was a soft knock at the door. A young man in scrubs walked in. "Transport," he said. "Let's get you into a more comfortable room." He wheeled in a transport bed to get Poppy onto.

"No, we're good. Hopefully we can get some sleep in our room. Thanks Lexi," he said, pulling her back in for another quick hug.

"Of course. Call me first thing in the morning."

Lexi and Liam made their way out of the room into the sterile hospital hallway. She stopped and took a deep breath and looked into Liam's eyes for the first time. She looked like she was exhausted and had been crying.

"I have a car here. Why don't we let it take us back to your house? We'll get you back here tomorrow to get your car."

She nodded. "Yeah, that sounds good."

Once they were in the car headed back to Mystic Falls, her head hit his shoulder and she was out. He pulled his phone out, it was almost two. It had been a long day that definitely hadn't turned out the way he thought it would. But right now, he was going to get her home and settled. Then tomorrow he would talk to her about Jacinda to see if anything needed to be smoothed over. But for right now he was happy to have her close again. Depending on what she wanted, he was hoping they could be close all the time.

Chapter 30

Lexi

Lexi stretched in bed. The sun was coming in through the cracks in her blinds. She was still trying to put together the pieces of yesterday as she woke up. Remembering Josh and Poppy were still in the hospital, she bolted up to check her phone. It was only eight and everything was okay. She didn't have any messages either, no news was good news on that front.

"Is everything alright?" Liam said, his voice still rough with sleep. His hand rubbed her back.

"Yeah. I just got scared that I slept through Josh trying to call, but we're good."

Liam snuggled her as she laid back down, holding her close to his chest. And she happily let him, happy to be here with him.

"It means a lot to me that you came last night."

He stroked her arm and pressed a kiss to her temple. "Of course, gorgeous. I came as soon as I got your message."

"I'm sorry I missed your concert. I got the text from my brother right after the opening act. I didn't even get to see you." She turned in his arms with a pout on her lips.

"Don't worry about that," he said as he kissed her fore-head. "There'll be other concerts." He got situated with her head resting on his chest. "I was worried about you last night. I'm glad they're both okay."

"Me too," she said, tracing the tattoo on his chest. "Thank you for coming."

"I would do anything for you, Alexis Turner. I love you."

Her head picked up quickly from her chest "What?"

"I love you," he said plainly, as if it were nothing at all.

Her heart pounded in her chest. Sometimes she still couldn't believe it. After everything she had gone through, she would never have believed she was here, in love with a superstar.

"I love you too," she answered back.

Then that grin found his face, the grin that lit up arenas, but right now, was just for her. He rolled her onto her back and settled between her legs.

"Say it again!"

"I love you, Liam Sheffield." She barely had enough time to get out the last word before his mouth came crashing down on hers. God, she loved kissing him. She could kiss him forever, and she just might. Liam started to kiss down her neck and thank fuck, she was ready for this. She had missed him in the week they were apart. Yes, she was now well acquainted with sex via FaceTime, but nothing beat in person.

"Is this okay?" he asked. The words were said between reverent kisses on her neck. "It's alright if you're not in the mood."

"I'm very much in the mood," she said, as she fisted her hand in his hair, pressing him closer. He let out an approving growl and nipped at her neck. She could already feel her desire pooling deep inside of her. She needed him, needed this. His hands began to explore her body more urgently, helping her out of her pajamas. He kissed her again, his tongue dancing with hers as his hands found her breast. There would be time for lazy morning sex like they'd had in his penthouse, but they didn't have that kind of patience today.

"Please Liam, I need you." Her hands found the waistband of his boxers and she pushed at them. He slid them off and nestled himself right between her legs. Sliding a hand between them he slipped his fingers into her folds. His forehead dropped to hers and he groaned.

"Oh my god, you're so wet. Do you have a condom?"

Her heart dropped and she shook her head. "I have an IUD," she panted.

"I've been tested, it's your call," he said as his fingers explored her and pushed into her core.

"Please Liam," she moaned as she ground into his hand. She had never been this brazenly desperate with anyone before, but she needed him. She loved him and she needed this.

His thumb began to rub her clit and she felt her climax building. He lifted his head and looked at her and smiled that fucking smile and she broke. He kissed her while she came on his hand, and she didn't think life could get any better. That was until he slid his hand away and pushed inside of her. His mouth still connected to hers and he slowly began to thrust. At first, his movements were slow and indulgent. He slowly sipped at her mouth while moving inside her. She slid her hands around to his perfect ass and gave it a squeeze. He groaned and broke the kiss and started thrusting into her with more purpose.

He pressed his forehead to hers and used an arm to

anchor himself as his rhythm increased. Lexi cried out on the verge of coming again.

"I love you so much," he said and kissed her.

At the utterance of those words her climax came barreling through her. He gave a few final thrusts before he went rigid, and she felt him pulsing inside her.

"I love you too," she said with one last kiss as he pulled out of her and fell to her side.

"When do you need to get back to the city?" she asked, praying she at least had the day with him, maybe another night.

"I don't," he said nonchalantly.

Lexi turned quickly in bed looking at him. "What do you mean you don't?"

"I'm done with the tour. My contract is up with that label and I'm taking some time to figure a couple things out," he said with a smile.

"Are you serious? You can stay for a couple of days?"

"I'm hoping to stay a little bit longer, but that's a conversation to have after coffee and breakfast."

"Are you serious?" she squealed. She was giddy. She couldn't recall the last time she was giddy. Nope. She was pretty sure this was the only time she had ever felt giddy like this before.

He just smiled that amazing smile of his at her and nodded. She reached up and pulled his head down to her for one big kiss.

"Let's go make some breakfast so we can talk about these plans of yours."

She shot out of bed naked as a jaybird and began searching for the pajamas that had been thrown off. Liam just sat up in bed and watched her.

"You're awfully cute, you know that?"

"Get dressed," she said, tossing him his boxers.

They made their way to the kitchen to scrounge up breakfast.

"Okay, you make some coffee and I'll make some breakfast if you have any food in here," he opened her refrigerator clearly expecting to find it bare, but she had gone shopping. "Look at you, with a fully stocked fridge. I can make you a proper breakfast with this."

She smiled at the familiarity he had with her shopping habits. It's the little things that make her unreal relationship feel grounded.

In no time they both were sitting at the table, eating omelets and drinking coffee.

"So, tell me these plans of yours," Lexi said, unable to wait any longer.

"My plan is that I don't really have any set plans. I just want to be with you."

"Look at that, I want to be with you too! We have so much in common."

"Good. I meant what I said upstairs. I love you. I'm with you and we're going to make this work if that's what you want."

"That's very much what I want." There were tears burning her sinuses, but she wasn't going to let them out. She had cried enough yesterday, but she was so happy.

"I've been looking at property around the Mystic Falls area. I hope that isn't too presumptuous," he said, sounding a bit uneasy.

She held his hand as he discussed the properties.

"One's a farmhouse. It would need some major renovations and we could convert the barn to a recording studio. The other is a couple of acres we could build on, make it whatever we want."

"You're serious about this?" She asked. She had dreamed about this. Things were still so new with them, but in a way, it felt like they had been together for years. Their comfort level and level of commitment was not something that grew in a mere two weeks, but here they were. This was crazy.

"I think I am," he said, his fingers lightly grazing over her knuckles.

"This is crazy," she said plainly.

Liam nodded his head and gave her a soft smile. "If it is too fast, we can wait, but I hope you won't mind me being around a lot. I have no desire to go back to the city and spend time away from you."

"Now that I can easily agree to." She would easily agree to the rest, but it all just felt so quick. But if he wanted to be here, who was she to say he didn't belong here?

Since her time in New York, she had been thinking. She liked her job at the inn, but it wasn't fulfilling. It wasn't her life's work, and she was tired. The thought of touring the world with Liam but having Mystic Falls as their home base was an amazing idea. She had worked her ass off taking care of her and Josh for almost twenty years. She had been in survival mode for so long she didn't even know how to be any other way.

When Liam had asked her what she would do, she wasn't lying when she said she would rest then see the world. Resting shouldn't be a privilege. Resting should be a part of life, but the hand that Lexi had been dealt just didn't allow for it.

She should have hobbies and friends and passions, all she had was the inn. She, of course, had her brother, but he was making his life his own, and it was time Lexi did the same.

Maybe it was time to take some time off. Learn what it's

like to be cared for by another person, build a relationship with her brother as an equal and not a caregiver, and rest. She had been fighting burnout for most of her life. If she gave into it one inch, it would pull her down, but maybe she should let it. All Liam wanted to do was shut the world out and relax for a while... Maybe they could do that together.

"So, I told you when I started at the inn, right?"

"Yeah, when you were in high school."

"Yeah, I've been there for going on twenty years. I'm only thirty-three and I've never taken a single vacation day until the past week."

He nodded slowly, his eyebrows tight with concern. The gut instinct to stop and not say this was strong. Her gut reaction to buckle down and do what needed to be done washed over her, but it was time. She was ready to be done.

"Part of me is thinking about taking a leave of absence from work for a while. A very long while. I hadn't allowed myself to think about it, but if you are thinking about relocating here, maybe I could."

"I would love nothing more than to be the reason you finally get to rest. I want to take care of you. I want to live a quiet life with you here in the Mystic Falls and have you on the road when I'm touring. We can travel, and this time, see more than just the inside of a hotel room. You have become my muse. The more time I spend with you, the more music I feel. I won't stop working, but if you want to take some time to figure out who you are and what your life looks like out of survival mode, let me help you."

She released a shaky breath. It was a scary thing to want, but she was ready. It felt anti-feminist to want to quit her job and be taken care of by this man, but she had worked her whole life. It was time for rest, and he could help. There had to be more to life than just working yourself to the bone, giving everything you have to merely surviving.

"We don't have to decide anything today, or even this week. Just let me stay here for a few days and we'll figure it out."

"Wouldn't you rather stay at the inn? It's much nicer than this place."

"I'll stay anywhere you're staying. At some point, I'll take you home and show you where I lived. In fact, my nephew's fifth birthday is next week, and I didn't think I would be able to go, but it's looking like I can now. Would you go with me?"

She nodded quickly.

"Now when you see my mom's house, just know that's not how I grew up. I bought her a fancy house as soon as I could."

"If it is okay with you," he continued. "I can get a keyboard set up and find a little corner to work on my music. Staying at a small inn isn't ideal for an artist who likes to write music at three in the morning."

"That is a valid point, there may be some complaints."

"So, I'm here. We can look at the property or the farm-house. We can do whatever you want. Work at the inn if it fulfills you, quit if it doesn't. Sleep for days and I'll wake you up for food and orgasms as needed."

"You joke, but you have no idea how good that last one sounds," she said with a chuckle.

He gripped her hand with a bit more pressure. "Then it's not a joke, Lexi. Burnout is a real thing. It can take time to recover from. Let me take care of you. It is okay to let go, to let others take care of you."

At the utterance of those words, big fat tears slid down her cheeks. Letting go sounded so good.

"Oh god, don't cry," he said, raising his hands to wipe her cheek.

"Okay. Maybe I could take a short leave of absence," she said, just testing out the words. It was all so new, but she knew it's what she wanted.

"A leave of absence or leaving entirely. I'm not one of the rock stars who has spent his entire fortune on cars and coke. Drugs were never my thing, and the only extravagance I have is spoiling my family. I assure you, I have enough put in smart places to take care of us for as long as we need. And I have a feeling my next album is going to be pure magic with a muse like you."

"Sometimes I'm still so scared I am going to wake up and this will all be a dream."

"It's not a dream, but sadly I can't assure you this will be without its hardships. We do need to talk about the photo that was leaked and what will happen when they find you, because they will find you. That's the reality of being my partner."

She nodded. This part was less pleasant, but he was worth it. "Okay, hit me with it."

"I think we should steer clear from the city for the time being. I'll have a keyboard, my guitars, and some clothes delivered here, and we'll just live our lives here for a while. The paparazzi will come and take their pictures, but they won't stay long. Living here will be a good way to stay out of the public eye. I just need you to promise me one thing," he said.

"What's that?"

"Trust how beautiful I think you are and never read the comments."

"Done!"

He stood up and pulled her into a hug. "I love you so much, Lexi."

"I love you too."

His mouth crashed on hers and she kissed him right back. He was her person, and she couldn't be happier.

Her phone dinged on the table. While she was tempted to just let it go, Poppy was still in the hospital, and it was probably Josh.

> Josh- They are discharging Poppy soon. She is doing better and the baby looks great so we are good to head home.

> Lexi- I'm so glad. Do I need to come and get you?

> Josh- If you don't mind. Our car is totaled.

> Lexi- Of course, we'll be there soon.

> Josh- Ok just text when you get here.

"Poppy is being discharged from the hospital. We have to go get them," Lexi said as she turned to go up the stairs to get dressed.

"I'm glad she's okay. I'll order a car. I need to get one of my own here," he said as he pulled out his phone.

"Wait a minute. I totally forgot I didn't drive home." She picked up her phone again and started texting.

> Lexi- My car is still at the hospital in the emergency room parking. I came home with Liam. Do you just want to drive my car? You have a key right?

> Josh- Yeah, that worked out perfectly.

> Lexi- I'll come get it later today and bring over some dinner, sound good?

Josh- Sounds perfect, see you then.

"Okay, we're good. Josh is going to drive my car home. We'll go over there tonight and take them dinner."

"What is it you plan on taking them, gorgeous? Lean Cuisine or breakfast food because that's about all you got."

She looked at him with fake offense. "Of course not! I will be picking up food from the diner."

"Or I could cook."

"You cook?"

"I know my way around a kitchen."

"You're perfect. That settles it. You're never getting rid of me."

"Is that all it took?" He asked, bringing her in his arms again and pressing a kiss to her lips. "Let's get some groceries and once we have your car back, I'll send my driver back to the city. I don't think I'll need it. I'm ready for a summer in Mystic Falls with my girl. Bring on the festivals and the cookouts and the hikes by the waterfall."

"That sounds perfect."

Chapter 31

Lexi

Later that evening, Lexi helped Liam pack up dinner. He had made some amazing carne asada and rice and all the fixin' to make tacos. It smelled delicious. Lexi was thanking her lucky stars he knew how to cook. She would gladly do the dishes if he cooked like this. Men making delicious food for her was something she was glad would stay the way it was. They packed the food into the back of Liam's car service and headed over. After they got the food in, Liam said goodbye to his driver and sent him back to the city. Things felt pretty final when that happened.

Poppy and Josh were thankful for the meal. The four of them sat around the dining room table eating tacos and rice. The banter was easy. They treated Liam like he was one of them. Poppy and Josh were two of the friendliest people that Lexi had ever known. Poppy had been a bit starstruck the first time she met him, but now she was just seeing him as part of the family, and that settled something even deeper in her soul.

Lexi didn't have any family outside of Josh, and she had

been distancing herself from Josh. She thought since he got married, he needed independence. She didn't want him to feel like he needed to include her because he felt bad for her. But now she was beginning to realize it didn't have to be that way. She wasn't a burden. He could invite her to things because he enjoyed her company. And yes, maybe on some level he wanted to bring her along with him into Poppy's family, so she wasn't alone. But what was wrong with that? Every family looked different. The Smith family had always been so full of love. It was okay if Lexi let them in.

The thought that Lexi might go from having no family to two families began to overwhelm her.

Josh looked at her and quirked his head. "Are you okay?"

"Yeah, I'm just so glad you and Poppy are okay. And I'm so happy I'm going to be an aunt. We are going to spoil them, aren't we?" she said to Liam.

"If my niece and nephews are any indication, there will be definite spoiling," Liam said, taking her hand.

"So, you guys are doing this then?" Josh asked, looking between them.

"We are," Lexi said, looking over at Liam who was smiling warmly at her. "We're not quite sure what this looks like, but we are definitely doing it." Liam winked at her, and her heart was in danger of exploding. Her heart had never been this full. Her brother now had an amazing support in his life and the start of the little family he always wanted. And then there was Liam, who was offering love and a life they could make their own. It might take some time for her to trust this, but she knew deep down these people weren't going anywhere.

"I'm really happy for you, Lex," Josh said with a smile.

"Right back atcha, little brother."

They chatted and finished their meal. Lexi and Liam cleaned up while Josh helped Poppy upstairs to get some rest. They packed up all the leftovers, put them in their fridge, and headed home.

Once they were back in Lexi's house, they settled in for the night in front of the TV with a tub of ice cream and a couple spoons. In moments like this, Lexi could forget she was dating The Liam James. In this moment, watching reruns of Buffy the Vampire Slayer, and cuddling on the couch, he was just Liam Sheffield.

Their whirlwind love affair had turned both of their lives upside down and had set them right here in this incredible moment. Neither of them had felt normal for a very long time. Neither of them wanted to run from their past, but they were looking forward to the future that lay ahead of them.

"Hey, do you want to show me the paperwork for the house or the land? I would love to start moving on getting out of this house. That is if you were wanting me to move in. I know that's a lot to assume--"

She was cut off by his mouth on hers, his tongue sweeping into her mouth. Her heart started pick up. The desire she felt just kissing him would never stop surprising her. But it went as soon as it came. She laughed at him as he nearly jumped off the couch to go and get the papers from the kitchen table.

He returned with the folders and spread them out on the coffee table in front of them. Lexi looked at the farmhouse. It was nice, and the barn could be good for Liam, but then she looked at the land. There was a perfect clearing for a house and that clearing wasn't far from the falls. The falls where her mother had taken them camping. The falls where she and Josh had escaped together when things got too hard. The falls where she had first decided to confide in Liam.

It was a blank slate. A place for them both to get what they wanted and exactly what they needed, next to this beautiful natural space that held such meaning to them. The choice was easy.

"The falls," she said quietly.

"Yeah. We build our dream home next to the falls," he agreed softly next to her, as his arm fell around her waist and drew her to him.

She looked over at him, his face so close to her she couldn't help but reach out and cup it. His stubble scratched her fingers and he smiled at her warmly. The smile lines that bracketed his eyes pulled her attention to his warm brown eyes. She smiled and gave a little chuckle.

"What is it?" he asked as he turned his head to kiss the hand cupping his face.

"I just love you so much." And the honest truth of that statement settled into her. Their romance had been a breathtaking all-consuming love, but in this moment their love felt tender and fond and warm and perfect.

"I love you too. I'm so excited to be starting this next chapter with you. Here's to us!" he said, digging into the tub for another spoonful of ice cream.

"To us," Lexi joined him with her own spoonful of ice cream. They gave a cheers with their spoons. They laughed and settled back into the couch because they were in no hurry. There was time to figure the details out and that time would be spent together. Neither of them could think of anything better.

Epilogue

Two Years Later

There was a knock at the door. Lexi was already on her way down the stairs. She had just finished getting ready. They were having a small going away party tonight. She opened the door and there stood her brother and a very pregnant Poppy.

"I told you guys you don't have to knock," she said, pulling her brother into a hug.

"I can't believe you are going to be gone for eight months," Josh said, holding her in the hug.

"I know, I'm excited though. So is Liam. This is his first big tour since we got together. The album is doing great, and the tour sold out. We're stretching it out so we can do some exploring."

"I'm so happy for you. So happy and not at all jealous," Poppy said, hugging her too.

"Don't worry. We'll be home for the holidays. I'm so sad

to miss this little one's entrance," Lexi said, reaching down to touch Poppy's belly. Lexi would never just touch anyone's pregnant belly, but Poppy had told her it was alright. Much to Poppy's own surprise, she loved being pregnant, and this was number two. Poppy had given birth to the most beautiful baby girl last year. She had Poppy's dark hair but Josh's sparkling blue eyes. Even as a baby she had been breathtaking, and Lexi wasn't even a baby person.

She had been relieved to find out that Liam didn't particularly want his own kids either. They were both content to spoil their nieces and nephews. Lexi and Liam hadn't even gotten married, and it wasn't something they were rushing to do. They were deeply in love and committed to one another. They didn't need a piece of paper to prove it.

"Good, because Lily wouldn't stand for a Christmas without her favorite aunt and uncle," Poppy said with a smile.

"You better not let Sam catch you saying that. I think that is them coming down the drive," Lexi said.

As the night went on, all their new friends came for dinner and board games. Their house was nicer than anything Lexi ever would have dreamed of living in, but nothing extravagant, as people would assume Liam James lived. It was just a home. One with an entire basement full of instruments and a recording studio that led out to the beautiful pond with a porch swing where Liam wrote some of his best music. But a regular home, nonetheless. On the other side of the pond was a trail to the waterfall. It was perfect.

Later that night, after everyone went home, it was time to start packing. They would be leaving in a few days.

Lexi had quit her job not long after she and Liam got

together. After a month off, she returned to find and train her replacement, and then left. At first, she didn't know what to do with herself. Working had always been a big part of her identity. It took a while to get used to, but it felt nice to stop.

She took time to explore who she was and what she liked because she didn't really know. They had a craft room full of things she had tried, and some she even liked. She never did cook, still hated that, but she loved to garden. She spent time planting flowers and taking care of their space. She loved when Liam would strum his guitar on the porch swing while she worked with her hands in the dirt. That was her happy place.

"Well, gorgeous, why don't we call it a night? I have an early meeting with Sue."

Lexi yawned while she put the last glass into the dishwasher. "That actually sounds really great. I'm tired." She stretched and turned around to find Liam looking at her. He had a look in his eyes that she knew well. That look told her that she wouldn't be sleeping for a while. As tired as she was, she could definitely rally for whatever he had in mind.

"Hopefully not too tired," he said, walking over and putting his hands on either side of her, pinning her to the counter. His mouth claimed hers and her hands ran up his arm and neck until they were fisted in his hair. His kiss traveled down her neck, and he gently bit her.

"Not anymore," she said breathlessly.

"Get upstairs," he said, pulling himself off her.

She quickly turned on the dishwasher, then headed out of the kitchen. But not before Liam smacked her ass, the stinging pain and the loud smack making her gasp.

"God, I love your ass," he said, watching her walk away.

"Are you coming? Or do I need to get started without you?" She said over her shoulder with a mischievous smile.

"Don't you fucking dare," he said, still admiring her as she walked away.

And while the fear of waking up from the dream of Liam James had stopped a long time ago, Lexi still felt the need to pinch herself from time to time. She still couldn't believe this was her life. She got to spend her time finding things that fulfilled her, spend her days with her best friend and biggest supporter while seeing the world or just hanging out at home, and she got to spend her nights in bed with that same person who she loved more than she had ever even dreamed possible. It was a happiness she could feel in her bones. She only hoped that Liam felt the same way. But she could tell he did, and that was probably the best part of all.

Afterword

This book is my love letter to rest. When COVID hit, I was one of those people whose life came to a screeching halt. There were no more dance classes, piano lessons, play practices, trips to the grocery store, endless hours in the car chauffeuring everyone everywhere and trying to get everything done in the few spare moments I had left.

I was forced into a slower pace, and it changed my life. I had more time for personal exploration and to figure out the things in life that brought me joy and the things in life that were just a headache. I chose to do things because I enjoyed them. I stopped doing things those I felt I was supposed to.

When I was able to slow down, I realized how hard I had been trying to live a life that I wasn't built for. Through that experience, I learned the value of rest.

Now I rest when I can, and I hold boundaries for my time.

A good nap is never a waste of time. A cup of coffee on your porch listening to the rain is a gift. A board game with your family is a core memory. Taking time to take care of yourself, even if it is watching the same episode of New Girl for the twentieth time is okay.

Rest. You don't need permission.

Spotify Playlist

I have a playlist I listen to when I am working on books. I thought you might like to see.

Here's the one for Lexi Lets Go (no surprise at the amount of Harry Styles on the list.)

Sign of the Times - Harry Style
Where You Lead - Carole King
She Used to Be Mine - Jessie Mueller
As It Was - Harry Styles
9 to 5 - Dolly Parton
Falling - Harry Styles
From the Dining Table - Harry Styles
Adore You - Harry Styles
Matilda - Harry Styles
Till We Both Say - Nicotine Dolls
What Makes You Beautiful - One Direction
Sweet Creature - Harry Styles
Girls Crush - Harry Styles
Love of My Life - Harry Styles
Lover - Taylor Swift

A Thousand Years - Christina Perri
Till Forever Falls Apart - Ashe, FINNEAS
To Make You Feel My Love - Adele
First Times - Ed Sheeran
Pointless - Lewis Capaldi
I Am Yours - Andy Grammer
If I Could Fly - One Direction
Pancakes for Dinner - Lizzy McAlpine

Also by Mary Warren

A Highlander for Hannah - *Mystic Falls Book 1*

Hannah is ready for some life changes. After visiting a Ren Faire, she preforms a love spell and the next morning wakes up to a highlander from 1745 in her barn, not quite the life changes she had in mind.

Spotlight on Poppy - *Mystic Falls Book 2*

Poppy is ready to jump start her life that seems to have stalled out when she gets a love spell from the same witch that just brought her best friend love. When a broadway star rolls into town, she things her dream is coming true, but her love has been under her nose the whole time.

Coming September 29th 2023

Magic in the Mountains

A new series about a woman down on her luck, who Bridget takes under her wing and helps her find the protection of a gentle giant who just happens to be a bear shifter

Coming Winter 2024

Reclaiming Kate

Mystic Falls book 4

Katie McPhee's family is a hockey family. Her twin brother even plays for the Glendale Magic. He comes home for the winter festival and brings his teammate home. Kate vowed to never date hockey players, but Wes Darling is trying to change the score.

Acknowledgments

There are many people to thank, but as always I have to thank Will, my wonderful partner, who helps to ensure I always get enough rest, even if he sometimes has to make me.

Thank you to all the wonderful beta readers, your feedback helped to make Lexi and Liam my favorite story yet.

Thank you to Lexi at Morally Gray Edits for the hours spent editing and listening to me and answering all my questions. I love working with them.

And of course, Leni Kauffman, my book covers are a work of art and Leni always does an amazing job.

And now... I'm going to go take a nap.

About the Author

Mary Warren lives in Illinois with her family. When she's not writing stories of fat women, she's reading them and advocating for better fat representation. Mary founded Fat Girls in Fiction, pointing out positive fat representation for femmes and non-binary people in books. This project became a community and is something she is immensely proud of and happy to be working on.

For updates subscribe to my newsletter.
Or follow on TikTok or Instagram